The Prince of Denial

Also by Doug Wilhelm

True Shoes
The Revealers
Falling
Alexander the Great: Master of the Ancient World

Choose Your Own Adventure books
Curse of the Pirate Mist
The Underground Railroad
The Gold Medal Secret
Shadow of the Swastika
Gunfire at Gettysburg
Search the Amazon!
The Secret of Mystery Hill
Scene of the Crime
The Forgotten Planet

The Prince of Denial

Doug Wilhelm

Interior illustration by Sarah-Lee Terrat

LONG STRIDE
BOOKS

Montpelier, Vermont

Published by Long Stride Books
Montpelier, Vermont
www.longstridebooks.com

Visit Doug Wilhelm on the web at
www.dougwilhelm.com

Library of Congress Control Number: 2013911123

ISBN-13: 978-0-9857836-3-1 (Long Stride Books)

Printed in the USA

The world breaks every one and afterward
many are strong at the broken places.

Ernest Hemingway
A Farewell to Arms

Part One

1.

"*Gas Attack*," I said. "By Mustafa Binyu."

"*Yellow River*," said Oscar. "By I.P. Freely."

"That is *so* old."

He grinned. "It is a classic."

"Okay, okay," I said. "*Cliff's Edge*. By Hugo Furst."

"*We Raced a Tiger*. By Claude Bunz."

Sitting in the tree on a thick lower branch, feet dangling below us, we recited the titles, saying our game.

"*Molehills into Mountains*," said Oscar. "By Phil D. Cleevidge."

"*Ball Three*. By Juan Ekstra."

"Hey, check it out — I got a new one."

"Okay ..."

"*Green Smears*," he said. "By Flicka T. Pick."

I was fidgeting, nervous. "I should go," I said. "And that's just gross."

"So? Gross is beautiful. Yo, say it *loud* — I'm disgusting and proud!"

"Oscar, I need to go."

"Aw, come on, man, we haven't done this in *forever*. Okay, I got one more. This one's better. Really."

He peered at me hopefully from under his hat, the black straw fedora he wore everywhere but in school (and he'd wear it there, too, if they let him). One time I told him the hat made him look like he was auditioning for some new boy band. He could be the group's funny, slightly pudgy black kid. "Hey man, whatever," he'd said. "My hat's my *style*."

Now he grinned. I knew he wanted this to be fun but I couldn't help it, I needed to get home. I grabbed a branch to swing down. His hand came out to stop me.

"This one's great," he said. "Ready?"

I shrugged. I nodded. Oscar raised his hand and gazed at it, like he was about to recite Shakespeare. The leaves all around us were glowing bright orange. It was almost October, bright and sunny beyond our tree.

"*The Groping Hand*," he said. "By Mister Butt Tried."

I smiled; I couldn't help it. Oscar punched air — "yes!" — then he wobbled, and grabbed the branch. "Does that make the Modern Library," he said, "or what?"

"I don't know. It's not *quite* ..."

"Yeah, I know — it's not exactly ... How 'bout *The Phantom Hand*?"

"*The Shadow's Hand.*"

"*The Empty Hand.*"

"*My Hand Is Empty*," I said, solemnly. "By Mister Butt."

Oscar was quiet. Then he whistled.

"That's beautiful, man. That's just ... beautiful."

"Great, okay. Later." I turned on my stomach and lowered myself to the bottom branch.

"Aw, come on, Casey! Stay more than five minutes."

I dropped to the ground and looked up. He was sitting hunched over up there like a large, unhappy bird. With a hat.

I did feel bad.

"I just have to go, okay?"

"No, man, it's ridiculous. You *never* hang out anymore."

Oscar dropped to the bottom branch. It swayed. "I'm coming over to your place," he said. "Right now. Let's go."

"Not today," I said quickly. "Tomorrow maybe."

"That's what you always say, Casey. I don't get it — why can't I come over? Why won't you do stuff after school any more?"

"I don't know. I just ... it's not a good time."

"Hey, come on — it's a *great* time!"

Oscar waved at the world past our tree. "We're seventh graders now, Case — we got *choices*. We could play Hoop Jam or Storm of Battle, at my place or yours. We could go downtown and read comics at the store till they throw us out, like the old days. We could watch old shows on TV, man. *Boy Meets World*!"

"Sorry, Oscar. I just have stuff to do."

"What, like homework? You can do that later. Like a *normal* kid."

"Not that."

"Then what? I don't get it, man. Like what?"

I shrugged, turned away, started walking. "I'll see you," I said without looking around.

"Don't be so sure!" he called from inside the tree. "I might be *busy*!"

It was two blocks to my house. I started running the last part, then I slowed down so no one would think anything was wrong. I got to the driveway at a fast jerky walk. I never should have fooled around. I shouldn't have. I didn't know if there was still time.

I hauled the two empty garbage cans up the driveway, setting them by the side door into the garage. The only remote for the big garage door was in my dad's car; I kept asking him to get another one, for me, but he hadn't remembered. So I grabbed an old chair that was still out here from when my mom used to sneak outside to smoke cigarettes, for her stress. I set it down by the corner of the garage, climbed up to stand on it and reached into the gutter, feeling in the slimy leaves until I found the key.

This was a great hiding place. I mean, if you wanted to break into our house and you were looking for the key, you wouldn't look up there because you'd think any key would wash down the drainpipe, right? But our gutters were all clogged with old leaves and stuff — they hadn't been cleaned since long before my mom and the Medalist left. So when I hid the key up there, it stayed. No one but me knew it was there.

I dragged the empty trash cans inside the garage, then hurried into the kitchen and got a grocery bag out of the drawer where I'd been stuffing them. In the living room it was murky; the shades were drawn and there was a stale, stuffy smell, which I always only noticed at first. I rushed around putting bottles in the bag, then brought the bag out to the garage, holding the bottom in case the bottles broke through. That did happen, once. I dumped the bottles in the recycle bin.

Then I finished picking up the living room. I put my dad's and my laundry in the washing machine, and I cleaned up the dishes from breakfast. I'd learned to leave the bowls and pan from our oatmeal soaking in water before I took off in the morning, otherwise the sticky dregs in them would turn to cement. I only had to have that happen once, just like I only had to try using dish soap once in the washing machine when we ran out of laundry detergent. Whoa.

It was important for me to have everything under control when my dad came home. I never knew how he would be, so everything had to be just right. That's why I was in a hurry, and why I was startled — and not too happy about it — when the phone rang.

This was the house phone. I don't have a cell. My dad says not yet.

"Hello?"

"*Hi*, Casey. It's Julie."

"Hello," I said, keeping it short. I like my aunt, but this was not a good time.

"My dad's not here," I said.

"Actually, I was looking for you. Have you got a second?"

"Well ... I've kind of got stuff to do right now."

"Okay, I won't take long. I was wondering if you and I could get together after school sometime soon. There's something I'd love to talk with you about."

"I usually come right home."

"I bet you could spare half an hour, though, couldn't you? It's kind of important."

I stood there and shook my head no.

"Casey? What do you say?"

"Well ..." I sighed. "I guess. Sometime."

"How about tomorrow?"

"*Tomorrow?*"

"It's important, Casey. It really is."

"Can't you talk to my dad about it?"

"Actually, no. I need to talk to you about it."

And I needed to go. "I ... guess so."

"Great. What if we meet at that ice-cream place near your school — what's it called?"

"Ike's?"

"That's it. That's a nice place, right?"

"I guess."

"I'll get us cones," she said. "Or, I mean, whatever you want."

"Well, okay, but ... I'll have to come home right after."

"I'll drive you," she said. "Three-thirty? See you then?"

"How about three?"

"I don't think I can get away that early. Three-fifteen? I *will* drive you home."

"Well ... I guess."

"All right, Casey. See you then and there. Thanks!"

I hung up quick, started throwing clothes in the dryer. The phone rang again.

I ran back and grabbed it. "*Hello!*"

A girl said, "Oh ... I'm sorry." It wasn't Julie. Her voice sounded shadowy.

"Is this ... um ... is this Casey?"

"Yes," I said, feeling rude.

"Well ... um ... this is Tara Kiernan."'

"Huh?" I thought, Tara *Kiernan?*

"Do you, ahm, know me?" she said. "I'm in social studies with you."

"Well, oh — I mean, sure," I said. "Sure. How ... how's it going?"

"All right," she said. Then, after a second: "You're ... probably wondering why I called."

"Well ..."

I couldn't *believe* she'd called. Tara Kiernan? First of all, she was supposed to be rich. Second, she was maturing. Physically, if you know what I mean.

Then it hit me. "Hey, is it about that Revolution thing?"

"Yes! I was ... just wondering if you would like to talk about the Boston project a little," she said. "I mean, to talk about some ideas, maybe."

It sounded almost like she'd written down what she was going to say, and was reading it. I couldn't believe it. Would Tara *Kiernan* be nervous? Why?

Okay, the Boston project. It was a study unit — you know, social studies and English and art, all mooshed together. We were supposed to partner with somebody, to make a final project using different media about Boston before the American Revolution. First we were supposed to do some reading and research, and everyone had to write an essay. I hadn't started thinking about any of it.

"I have *no* ideas," I said.

She laughed. "Neither do I."

"That's not too much to talk about," I said, then felt bad. "But we *could* meet. I mean, we're gonna have to think of something."

"Yes," she said. "That's right."

She had a soft voice. I guess she was waiting for me to say something more, and I was waiting for her to say something more. I got nervous.

"Why don't we ... maybe ... I don't know ..."

"I could meet tomorrow," she said, "if you could. After school."

"Oh, sure. And we could ... you know ... talk about it."

"I can bring a bunch of books I borrowed from the library," she said. "About the Revolution."

"Is *that* where they all went?"

She laughed again, but she sounded unsure.

"I ... didn't mean that," I said quickly. "Only as a joke."

"Yes. It was funny."

"I don't know why I said it. I haven't looked for any

books at all."

"Really, it was funny. Would you like to meet at the ice cream place?"

"Sure," I said. "I just ... I won't be able to stay too long."

"Oh — if you don't have time, it's really all right."

"No! I do," I said. "It's just ... I have these chores. At home. But I can definitely meet."

"All right."

I was *sweating*. Nothing like this had happened to me before.

"So, that's good," I said, pointlessly.

"I'll meet you at Ike's after school," she said. "I'll bring the books."

"Sure, okay. At what, like three?" We got out of school at 2:45. If you hustled you could make it.

"That would be fine," Tara said.

I heard the big garage door rumble up.

"Oh my god," I said. "I have to go!"

She was saying something as I hung up the phone.

I started tearing around the kitchen. I swiped the counter with a sponge, started emptying the dishwasher ... I should have done this! I shouldn't have messed around. I was shoving glasses into the cabinet when I heard my dad coming up the garage steps. Bouncy footsteps. A good sign.

Backed up against the counter, I turned and smiled.

As he came into the kitchen, he saw me and grinned. My dad has a great smile. He still has freckles, just like me.

"Caboose, my *boy!*" He set two paper bags on the counter. One was square and full. I was trying to see if the second one had any food in it. But I wasn't too worried. My dad was *happy*.

"How was school?"

"Good."

"Great. Hey, I got some stuff here. Thought we'd have sausage and peppers for dinner. How does that sound?"

"Great! That sounds great, Dad."

From the second bag he pulled out a long blue package of spaghetti, and a jar of our favorite sauce. "I got the good stuff," he said, winking. Next came Italian sausage, pink and brown under the plastic, and one green pepper, swinging in a plastic bag. My dad hardly ever bought more than what we needed for one or two meals at a time, but that was okay. This was fine.

He set the food on the counter, then reached into the full square bag, lifted out two six-packs and put them in the fridge. He pulled out a bottle and twisted it open with a *psht*.

"Aah," he said when he'd had some. He smiled. "So. Tell me what happened today."

"Not much."

"What'd you do after school?"

"Nothing. I saw Oscar."

"Oscar Terry! How is that old troublemaker?"

"He's okay."

"He still wear that hat?"

"Oh god," I said. "Always."

"It's dapper," my dad said as he drank some more. "A dapper hat."

"I guess."

He grinned. "Remember those patent-leather Jordans? From fifth grade?"

I had to laugh. "He called them O Force One," I said. "Like he could ever jump an inch."

"Maybe not — but the boy has style," my dad said. He nodded as he drank, then he set the bottle down. "You should have him over. He never comes over any more."

I looked down. I shrugged.

"No really," he said. "Tell him to stop by. Drop in for dinner sometime, like he used to do back in the day. Back in the frickin' *day*."

I looked up. My dad's face was turning red.

"Okay," I said.

"You tell him." He took a long drink.

"I will. Sure."

"Tell him to stop over. It's no problem. Nothing's *different*."

"It's okay, Dad."

"Did I say it wasn't? You just tell him. Say we're right here — you and me. Like always. Stop on by."

"Sure," I said. "No problem."

"Okay."

He set the bottle down again, and took a deep breath. His face was calming down. He took off his jacket, loosened his tie, started rooting around for pots and pans.

"Go do something fun, Case. Or homework. Got homework?"

"Yeah. A little."

"Well, go do it so you can relax later. I'll call you when dinner's ready."

"Okay, Dad."

I went into my room. I was supposed to be reading *Johnny Tremain*, this old-time book about a kid who gets mixed up with the radicals in Boston — they called themselves the Sons of Liberty — right before the Revolution starts. On the inside cover, the book has a pretty decent picture map of Boston the way it looked back then. I started thinking maybe we could make a display of old Boston, for the project, like a papier-maché layout or something. That would be combining media, right?

I could tell Tara about the idea. She might like it. I

could bring this book when I met her tomorrow. She might know how to do papier-maché. I still couldn't believe I was meeting with *Tara Kiernan*. I tried to picture her in my mind. I could, too. I felt sort of shaky.

After a few minutes I heard a click. It was a door opening, in the little hall next to the kitchen; it went out to the garage. I heard the thunk as the door closed.

I closed *Johnny Tremain*. Tonight, I told myself, I would start reading it for sure. Then I went into the kitchen, to finish cooking dinner.

3.

The sausages were sizzling and spitting in the pan. I
turned them over — they were brown on the bottom,
but not black. That was fine. I turned the sauce down so
it wouldn't spatter. A pot of water, for the spaghetti, was
almost boiling. Everything was good.

My dad and me, we do fine together. In a lot of ways
it's been better since Mom and the Medalist moved to
Maine. Right before the splitup it got fairly bad, like
things were frozen solid in our house. That's how it was
with my mom, anyway. Until almost the end, I don't
think my dad even noticed — which of course made it
worse. The two of them got so they weren't speaking to
each other at all, not in any unfrozen way; so when my
mom finally left last spring it was a relief.

And it worked out the way it should have. My mom
is used to taking care of everything and everybody,
but lately she's been more and more into the Medalist

and her shining career. The Medalist is my older sister
Shannon. She won the New Hampshire State Geography
Bee in fifth grade, and she's never been second place
in anything since. Girls' softball star pitcher, seventh-
grade district science fair gold medalist — that's when I
made up my personal name for her. Now she's a high-
school soccer starlet, as my mom never fails to mention
whenever we talk on the phone.

So anyway, this is fine. We paired up like we should
have. Shannon was supposed to spend a lot of time with
my dad in the summer and I was going to go be with
our mom, but we wound up only doing that for one
sad week in August. I wanted to be here and Shannon
wanted to be there, and our parents weren't sure about
anything so they let us decide. I do miss my mom, but
my dad needs me — and unless she's basking in the
spotlight, the Medalist is basically helpless. She doesn't
even pick up her own clothes. How's she supposed to
take care of him?

I've learned to do — well, a lot. And my dad and
I have the greatest plans. Next summer we're going to
go see the Red Sox at Fenway Park, which is such an
outstanding old ballpark, one of the best places I've
ever seen. I still remember, when I was younger, how
the field looked when we came up the ramp and I saw
it for the first time, the outfield grass perfect and almost
glowing, like a magic carpet with ballplayers. We ended

up not making it to Fenway this past summer, but we'll definitely go next season.

We were going camping together too, just us two, last summer after the split. Actually we did go camping, but my dad got upset the first night and he was sick the next morning, so we came back. But next summer we'll go for sure.

When basketball season starts, we're going to go watch the Big Green. That's Dartmouth College. It's not far away; that's where my dad went to school. (He's really smart.) He's told me stories about Big Green basketball, and football too. They used to be the Dartmouth Indians, but that was culturally insensitive so now they're a color. Which is fine with me! I can't wait to go.

The music came on loud, out in the garage. Sometimes my mom used to go stomping out there. She'd fling the door open and the music would surge in; then she'd slam the door and we'd hear her start yelling. No way was I going out there.

The green peppers were cut up on the counter. I tossed them in the pan with the sausages. This pan was still bluish and messed up on the bottom, from being left on the stove too long with food burning in it, but it works fine. We've got one saucepan that has a black crust of incinerated chili still welded to the bottom. I couldn't even chip that off with a screwdriver.

I remember those first few times when I'd be in my room and the house would start to smell funny. I'd say, "Dad? Hey, Dad?" Then I'd get up and open my door, and the hall would be full of smoke.

So I learned. I didn't know how to cook anything back then, not to mention what to do with incinerated pans. Now I've cooked hamburgers, hot dogs, mac and cheese from the box, spaghetti, chili, and scrambled eggs. In the morning I make oatmeal, the real kind. It settles our stomachs. Cooking's really not a problem, once you focus.

As I was stirring the peppers and sausage in the pan, the music stopped. The door to the garage opened, and my dad came in. I didn't look up. The refrigerator door opened. He glanced over, the rest of the first six-pack in his hand.

"That'll be done soon," he said about the food. I nodded. It would be. He went into the living room. I took a deep breath.

I heard the surge of voices as he switched on the TV, and the springy sound as he hit the couch. I had a feeling it was going to be a nice, quiet night.

4.

In school next morning, Tara glided past me in the hall. She smiled. I think I said hi.

I noticed how she walks. She holds herself really straight, almost like she's leaning back, and with each step her long, dark hair swings a little behind her. She looks, I don't know, dignified — and also kind of separate. Most seventh-grade girls go around in tight little gaggles, chattering and whispering and going "Oh my *god!*" for no apparent reason. Tara you'd only see alone.

I wondered if that's why she asked me to talk about doing the project. I'm by myself a lot, too.

At lunch, Oscar spluttered over his milk carton.

"Tara *Kiernan?*"

"Uh huh."

"But ..." He leaned across the table, eyes wide.

"She's like *mature*." He glanced down at his chest.

"I know."

"So. I mean ... what's she want with you?"

"She wants to partner."

"She *said* that?"

"For a *project*," I added quickly. "We're supposed to. For social studies."

"I like it," he said, leaning back. "Why yes, Ms. Kiernan, I'd be pleased to *partner* with you. Will you be coming to my place, or should I go to yours?"

"Your brain is diseased."

"Hah! My brain is *normal*," he said. "Do you *see* what an opportunity this is?"

"I think she might be shy. We're meeting for ice cream."

"Very nice. Be sure to get a double scoop."

"I'm gonna pour this over your head," I said, reaching for his milk.

"Hey — unhand the beverage! Don't you think *Double Scoop* would make a good title?"

"If we're doing porn."

"Why not? We'd get rich."

He bit into his bologna sandwich, and thoughtfully chewed.

"You know what? Something's different about that girl," he finally said. "You never see her with anybody. I wonder who she hangs out with."

"I really think she's shy."

"I heard she lives up on White Oak Heights," Oscar said. "Ever see the houses up there? They're like castles."

"So? She can't help it if she's got money."

"Yeah, but ... I mean, what's a person like that gonna have in common with little I-got-to-scurry-home-now Casey Butterfield? Hey, wait — maybe she hides out in her house, too!"

"Don't start with that. All right?"

"'Sorry,' she'll say — 'I can only stay five minutes. Can I have just a thimble of ice cream?'"

"Oscar, shut up, okay? You don't know ..."

"Oh, I get it — you *want* to hang out with *her*. You'll make time for a double *scoop*."

I stood up. "Will you *shut UP?*"

I yelled that, pretty much. People around us stopped and stared. Oscar looked up and blinked, and I kept on yelling:

"You think everything's a stupid fricking joke. Well, you know what? *You're* the stupid joke. It's you. And I'm *sick* of it!"

I know that didn't make sense — he was just being him; but it came boiling up out of me. He looked stunned, and hurt. People were starting to buzz. I whirled around and stalked out of the cafeteria.

I did not understand what had just happened. Oscar and

I had been friends since we were little kids, and we'd had fights before, but … what was *that* about?

I tried not to think about it.

As the end of school came closer, I got more and more nervous about seeing Tara. Then, when the last bell finally rang, Ms. Scarpino, my math teacher, stopped me before I could get out of her classroom. She wanted to talk about some homework I was supposed to bring in, that I had forgotten about — and now I was *late*. It was almost three!

When she finally let me go I rushed out of school and almost ran the several blocks there. Ike's is this cartoon-colored place, with giant ice-cream cones painted on the walls inside. I pushed open the glass door and looked around.

She was sitting in a booth. A pile of books was stacked carefully on the table in front of her. She looked up at me and smiled, but kind of unsurely.

"Hi," I said, coming up. I was trying to calm down and not sweat.

"Hi," she said.

"I'm a little late. I'm really sorry."

"That's okay."

Now I didn't know what to say.

She glanced across the booth from her. I got that I should sit down.

"So," I said, sliding in. "Did you have, like, a good

day?"

"Oh, it was pretty much okay," she said. "How was yours?"

"It was all right. Yeah." I nodded. "I mean, pretty much."

I nodded again. She nodded too.

"I got held up, though," I said. "After school. That's why I was late."

Her eyebrows went up. "You *did?*"

"Yeah. By a teacher. I was trying to get away but she wouldn't let me. Homework issue. It was awkward."

"It was ... oh!" A really nice smile spread over her face. "I thought you meant you got *robbed.*"

I looked at her, then realized how it had sounded. I thought of Ms. Scarpino saying "Stick 'em up!" — and I started *laughing.* Now Tara was laughing, too. Not giggling, either. She had a nice, soft laugh.

I hadn't laughed in a long time. It felt good.

We finally settled down. "Ah," I said, shaking my head. "Hah."

"Uh huh."

"That was *funny.*"

"Yes. A misunderstanding."

I looked at her. I nodded again. She nodded back. I said, "So."

She looked at her folded hands.

"So," I said. "So you like ice cream?"

"I do!"

"Okay! Great. Me too."

"Should we get some first?" she said. "I mean, before we get to work?"

"Yeah. I had an idea," I said.

She nodded, and waited. When I didn't say anything, she tilted her head and gazed at me. I got ... confused.

"Um ... well," I finally said, "you know ... I mean, we should definitely have ice cream." I sat there, nodding earnestly at her.

"I think we have to go to the counter," she said.

"Oh. *Yeah*." I started to laugh as we got up. "Geez," I said, shaking my head.

Just as we came by the front door it opened, and in walked my Julie. My aunt.

I froze.

"*Hi*, Casey," she said. "You're right on time!"

I suddenly, suddenly remembered.

Oh my god.

Julie turned to Tara. "Hello," she said cheerfully, sticking out her hand. "I'm Casey's Aunt Julie."

"I'm Tara." Very soft.

"Well," Julie said, turning to me, "shall we get a cone? I know you said you don't have much time, but how can we not have a *cone*? I personally am currently addicted to Deep Dark Mint."

She turned to Tara again. "I'd offer you one, Tara,

absolutely any other time — except right now I really need to talk with Casey alone. I hope you don't mind."

Tara looked at her, then at me. My mouth was open. Tara's back went stiff, but she was very calm. "Oh, that's fine," she said, smiling at Julie. I couldn't tell if she was upset.

"It was nice to see you," she said to me, and she turned to go.

"Ah — wait!"

I stepped outside with her, leaving my aunt standing on the other side of the glass.

"Oh my god, I'm *really* sorry," I said. "I think I have brain damage. My aunt called yesterday about meeting here — but then you called and we talked and I thought that was ... I mean it was great that you called, then my dad got home and stuff happened and I just ... oh my god I forgot she was coming. I *totally* forgot. I'm really sorry."

Looking down, she smiled, a little. "It's all right," she said.

"Maybe we could get together again? I mean, we could work on this thing," I said. "We really should. We've got to work with *somebody*."

She flushed.

"I didn't mean it like that," I said.

"It's all right."

"No. It's not. I'm really sorry. I definitely have brain damage."

She smiled at me. "No, you don't."

"But we *could* work on it. You know? I could meet you, or you could come see me. You could come anytime."

She nodded. "All right."

"Okay! Great. I'm really sorry. I mean about this."

"It's okay," she said. "I understand. I'd better get my books, though."

"Oh yeah! Sure."

I held open the door, and Tara stepped past me, going in. My aunt was standing in line at the counter, not looking at us, probably on purpose.

As Tara came back she was clutching her books to her chest. I was still standing there, holding open the door.

"See you," I said. I knew she felt bad; I could see the bashful look in her eyes. I couldn't stand that. "Sorry about my brain damage," I called out as she walked across the patio in front of the shop.

People were turning to look. Tara turned back, and smiled. Then she walked away.

"My," Julie whispered when I came to the counter. "What a *mature* young lady."

5.

Julie got that mint stuff. I got buttercrunch fudge swirl. I don't like mint.

My aunt is my dad's younger sister. She's an art teacher. They (my mom and dad) told us she was *wild* for a long time. She lived in different places, had different boyfriends; we hardly ever saw her. I don't think she's wild any more. She teaches in three different elementary schools, driving her old car from one to the other because none of them has the money for a full-time art teacher. She lives in a town near us, but we don't see her much. That's pretty normal. We don't see anyone much.

Julie sat down in a different booth from the one I'd been in with Tara. I went over to get my backpack, then sat across from her.

My aunt took a little bite from her cone. I was licking mine. "I know you're pressed for time," she said

— "so here's what I wanted to talk about."

She leaned over the table, like this was private.

"I'm worried about David," she said.

"Huh?"

"I am. I'm worried about your dad."

"Why? He's fine."

She looked at me closely. "I don't think he's so fine at all," she said quietly. "I think you probably know that better than anyone."

I wondered, staring at my cone: what *is* buttercrunch? Butter's soft, unless it's frozen. Do they just freeze it to make it crunch? Or what?

My aunt stuck her face down sideways, looked up in my eyes. "Casey? Hello?"

"Uh?"

"I know this is hard."

"No it isn't. It's fine."

"It isn't ... all right." She sat back, took a deep breath. "Look," she said. "I would like you and me — just you and me — to meet with someone. This is a person who can help your dad, and maybe help you too. I think it would really be ... Casey? Can you look at me? I think it's someone who could help you guys a lot."

I shook my head. "I can't."

"Why can't you?"

"I just can't."

She leaned closer. "Look. Casey. I know you love

your dad, and so do I. Couldn't we just meet with somebody who could help him? He could maybe help both you guys. I mean, why not?"

"Because we're fine, okay?" I stood up. "Everything's *fine*. There's nothing *wrong*." I handed her my ice cream. "Here."

She sat there looking at me, a cone in each hand. Hers had bites out of it, mine was licked smooth.

"Casey, please."

"No!"

I turned and walked to the door. I shoved it open and walked away.

My dad came home a little late, but jaunty and jovial. He didn't have grocery bags. He pulled a bottle from the fridge and clapped me on the back.

"Know what, Caboose? It's high time we celebrated."

"Celebrated what?"

"Life, Casey. Life! We're alive and we're lucky. We've got us, we don't need them. It's Friday, it's the weekend, I got paid today and *we're* going out to dinner. Put a jacket on, and let's hit the high road!"

When we left, a little while later, there were three empty bottles on the kitchen counter.

We went to the Jefferson Inn. The place has been around

since colonial times, I guess — it's got a bunch of rooms that have dark beams and fireplaces, with silvery antique mugs on the mantels and paintings of frowning old-time guys on the walls. We sat at a table in the room up front. *SportsCenter* was playing on the big TV above the bar.

When the waitress came, my dad ordered his drink; then he said, "And a Shirley Temple for my partner in crime here." He winked at the waitress, but I sank in my seat. A Shirley Temple is embarrassing. It's like a fake cocktail for little kids.

When our drinks came, my dad swallowed his. His glass had only ice when he waved at the waitress. I pushed my drink aside. My dad ordered another for himself without looking down from the TV.

The waitress glanced at my Shirley Temple. She was young and pretty, with dark hair like Tara's but in a long ponytail.

"Something different?" she asked quietly.

I nodded. "Ginger ale?"

She smiled, and went off.

I'd hardly tasted my ginger ale when my dad ordered again. A minute later, that glass had only ice left. The men at the bar were looking at *SportsCenter*. I wasn't sure if my dad was okay. When the waitress came by again, she had a tray full of drinks balanced on her hand. He reached out and grabbed her other arm.

"Sir?" she said, pulling away gently.

"I bet you have a sister," he said, not letting go. He gave her a sneaky smile. "I *hope* you have a sister."

"Sir ..." She was trying to pull free but he was holding her elbow.

"A little sister," he said. "For my partner in crime." He grinned at me like he hadn't already made that joke, three fast glasses ago. I stared at the sweaty drops on my ginger ale glass.

"Please, sir," she said. "I have tables. Please let go."

"See, now that's the trouble with life," my dad said. His face was turning red. "Let me tell you the trouble with life, 'cause maybe you don' know yet. You always have to *let* go."

"Sir. Please!"

My dad said, "You always gotta *let* ... GO!"

I looked up as he yanked her elbow hard. The tray on her other hand tilted, then everything on it came crashing and splashing down on our table and all over my lap. I was suddenly wet, and freezing cold.

The whole room went silent. Only the *SportsCenter* anchors kept talking.

The bartender, a big guy, came over. He didn't say anything, he just bent over and started picking up the empty glasses from my lap and the floor, and putting them back on the tray the waitress had set on our table. She helped, then she gave me a cloth to wipe my lap. Nobody said a word. My dad stared straight ahead, gripping his empty glass. Nobody but me looked at him.

I felt terrible for my dad. I wanted to say, "He's not really like this — he's just having a hard time right now," to the stone-faced bartender and our waitress as they worked without looking up. "He really didn't mean it," I wanted to say. "He just had too much too fast."

My dad stared straight ahead, like nothing was happening at all.

After they got done cleaning up and went away, the conversation around us slowly picked back up; but we just sat there. The bartender came back over and set a bill on our table, face down. My dad paid it with his credit card, then we got up and walked outside.

In the car he didn't say a word. All the way home he didn't say anything. I was so scared he was mad at me. I finally said, "I'm sorry, Daddy. I'm sorry." My voice was trembling. "I'm really sorry."

He didn't say anything.

He pulled into a convenience store, and came out with a twelve-pack. Those come in a box.

Later, it was quiet in our house. My dad was in the living room with the TV on. I'd had a can of spaghetti for dinner. I wanted things to stay quiet, so I was not happy in any way to hear a *tap tap* on my window.

I looked. Oscar was standing out there. (Our house is all on one floor.)

I slid the window open.

"This is not a good time," I whispered.

"Oh hey, no need to apologize," he said. "You were under a lot of *pressure*."

"What?"

"A guy doesn't get a sort-of-date with Tara *Kiernan* every afternoon," he said. "So what if he's a total jerk to his best and pretty much last remaining friend?"

He pulled himself up to squirm in through the window, like he used to. I shoved him back out.

"Hey!" Landing on his feet, he grabbed his falling hat.

"Shut *up*," I whispered.

He looked at me with his face scrunched up. "What is it with you, Butterfield?"

"You can't come in right now. And I can't talk right now."

"Why not?"

"I just can't."

"Why *not?*"

"Because my dad's sick. Okay? It's not a good time."

Oscar cocked his head. "Sounds like your dad's watching TV."

"So? Don't you ever watch TV when you're sick?"

Just then heavy, stumbling footsteps hurried up the hall. From the bathroom we heard the roar of someone throwing up.

Oscar's eyes got wide. I slammed the window closed, and went to help my dad.

6.

On Saturday morning I didn't want to get up. But then I heard sizzling. I smelled bacon.

I came in the kitchen and sat down.

"Hey," he said.

I stared at the floor. "Hey."

My dad slid a plate of pancakes and bacon in front of me, and a glass of orange juice. I stared at those. Then I started eating. It was good. He sat across the table, sipping his coffee.

I said, "Aren't you going to have any?"

"Nah." He shook his head, and winced. "Listen, I was checking the paper. Dartmouth football is playing Penn today. Home opener. Want to go?"

"Well ... yeah!"

He nodded, and smiled. "I thought you might. Okay, pal. The kickoff's at one-thirty, so we have time. Let's do the recycling first, then I need to do a small job around here. We'll get lunch near the stadium. How's that sound?"

"How 'bout lunch *in* the stadium? Do they have that?"

"Sure — dogs and burgers," he said. "Want that?"

"Absolutely."

"Eat up, then. I'll load the car for the dump."

We really like doing the recycling. Ever since I was little we've done it together. The dump is about a mile outside of town on a gravel road. You go through a gate, then there's a yard with green, covered dumpsters that have openings on the side, and signs that say Aluminum Cans, Milk Jugs, Green Glass, Clear Glass, Brown Glass. We have mostly glass, and I throw in the bottles.

"I remember when I had to hold you up so you could fling those," my dad said. "Now you almost have to bend down."

I was pitching them quickly, getting rid of them.

"You don't have to throw so fast," he said. "Watch your eyes."

"You always say that."

"Well, you always should."

I lofted in the last one, a thick brown bottle. It didn't bust. The big thick ones were tough.

Then we went to the hardware store. A lady was behind the counter. My dad seemed annoyed. He said, "Isn't Jim here?"

"He's not in this morning," the lady said. "Can I help?"

"I don't think so," my dad said. "I have something to ask him about."

"Well ... you could try me," she said.

My dad looked like he didn't want to. But finally he said we had a leaky faucet in the bathroom. I was surprised. I mean, I knew we had it, but I was surprised he was going to do something about it.

The lady said, "Is it the sink faucet?"

"No," my dad said, "the bathtub. The one for the shower and the tub."

She asked if it had two knobs, for hot and cold water, or just one. He looked at me. I said we had two knobs. It was the hot-water one that leaked.

The lady asked, Was it leaking below the handle, kind of seeping out? Yes, I said. That's right.

Was it an older-looking faucet? Well, not that old, but not new either.

She nodded. "Okay," she said to my dad. "First you need to take off the handle. There's probably a screw on top that you need to loosen. There may be a little cap you have to pry off first. Under the handle you'll see a brass nut. Try tightening that. If that doesn't stop the leak, you have to unscrew the nut, and unwind or dig out the packing twine at the base of the faucet stem. It's black and gummy, the twine — it has graphite on it, to make a seal. Once you get it out, you just wind on some new packing twine. I'll get you some. It's pretty much the same for all faucets."

She walked down an aisle, then came back and handed my dad a little clear-plastic box with gummy black string coiled inside it. But she seemed worried.

"Have you ever done this before?" she asked my dad.

"No, but it seems perfectly simple," he said, getting out his wallet.

"Well ... if the stem is corroded at all, the nut can be hard to take off. The nut and the stem are both brass — that's a soft metal. They can crack, or break. You *might* want to call somebody."

"I'll be fine," my dad said shortly. "How much is this?"

The lady shrugged, and told him.

When we got home, my dad was going down to the basement to get his toolbox when the phone rang.

He shook his head. "I'll get it. Typical timing, right Case?"

He picked up the phone in the kitchen and there was a silence. Then he said, "Hello Janet."

That's my mom. I had a prickly feeling.

"Yeah," he said. "*Two* goals? That's great. Tell her I said congratulations. Wish I coulda been there."

He listened again. "Yeah, I'm going to send it," he

said. "Yeah, I know. Soon as I have it, you'll get your bite."

His face was dark. I knew he had his paycheck, but he didn't like having to send her money. Especially when it was her that left.

"Listen, I know that's all you wanted to talk about," he said, "but would you mind saying hello to your son? Oh yeah, you *have* one of those. Here."

He held the phone out like it was toxic. I took it.

"Hi, baby!" my mom's voice said. "How are *you?* Your sister had a game under the lights last night. She scored *two* goals!"

"I'm fine, Mom."

"Isn't that amazing? She's only a sophomore and the new kid in school, but she's already a starting striker. She was so excited — and she really was the star of the game. How are *you?*"

"I'm fine."

"Now listen, baby," she said, her voice dropping low. "Are you taking care of your dad?"

"Yes."

"'Cause, you know, he needs you."

"I know."

"He really does. He needs you right now."

"I know."

"Well, okay, baby," she said, her voice bright and chipper again. "I hope you have some fun today — is it nice there?"

"I guess."

"'Cause it's just beautiful here — crisp and sunny. Of course *we're* going shopping. You know teenagers! They have to be there when their tribe's at the mall!"

"Have fun, Mom."

"You too, baby. Have a great day. I miss you!"

"I miss you too, Mom."

"Take care of your dad, now — really. And take care of yourself."

"Right."

"Bye now!"

As I hung up I heard the refrigerator door open and close behind me. Then I heard the *psht*.

I went into my bedroom, and lay on the bed with the door open. I heard my dad go downstairs, then he came back up with his toolbox clanking. He went by my door with the toolbox in one hand, a bottle in the other. The bathroom is next to my room. I heard him set his stuff down in there.

For a couple of minutes I heard clinking and tinkering. Then he said, "Come on. Dammit! Come *on*."

I sat up. It was quiet for a second — then I heard two ringy taps, like a hammer on metal. A harder tap. Another curse, then bang! *Bang!*

POW!

There was a hard thud, a bang and clatter like things were hitting the floor, and a sharp loud hissing sound. My dad came out of the bathroom; when he pounded by my door I saw that his sweatshirt was dark wet in front. The sound of spraying water was going full blast.

My dad stomped down the basement steps. There was a creaking sound, down there, and then the spraying stopped.

He came upstairs. I heard the refrigerator door open and close. Then the door to the garage opened and closed. In a couple of minutes, I heard the music come on loud out there.

There was dirty water all over the bathroom floor, along with dropped tools and the faucet handle. In the tub, in a layer of greasy, black-specked water lay a T-shaped metal thing. I picked it up.

It was the valve stem, with the brass nut still screwed to the end. Old black twine was wound around the stem, just like the lady said it would be — but the stem had cracked all the way to the nut, and almost half of it was gone. I figured he couldn't get the nut to loosen up, so he'd banged on the wrench handle so hard with his hammer that it cracked the valve stem, and the water pressure made the pieces shoot out. Or up.

I looked up. Right above the faucet there was a deep dent in the ceiling, with dirty wet stains all around it.

I sighed. I *knew* he didn't listen to that lady.

I turned on the faucet in the sink to start cleaning up — but all I got was a dry hiss of air. I realized he'd turned the water off.

So I started swishing a towel around in the mess on the floor, and wringing it out in the toilet. But the water was so dirty — it had specks and scraps in it, from the black twine and the broken plumbing — that the towel got all gray and greasy. I was smearing the gritty mess around more than cleaning it. My hands were numb. But I did the best I could.

I hung the ruined towel on the shower-curtain rod. I put the pieces of the broken stem together on top of the toilet tank. Then I went into the kitchen and made myself a sandwich.

The bread got smudged all over by my greasy, filthy fingers. So I went downstairs and found my dad's hand-cleaning goop, got myself pretty clean, then came back up and scooped the bread crumbs into my hand and into the garbage, so I wouldn't leave a mess.

I ate my sandwich, sitting in the kitchen. I watched the clock turn to 1:25, then to 1:30, then to 1:35.

Later in the afternoon my dad was in the living room, yelling at a football game on TV. I was in my room with the door closed. We had no water at all. I didn't know how to turn it on downstairs, and even if I did it would just make another awful mess.

It feels weird to be in a house without water. You get thirsty, but it's more than that. The whole place feels dry. I was sitting there, arms around my knees, trying not to hear or see anything, when the front doorbell rang.

Our doorbell hadn't rung in so long, I wasn't sure at first what it was. Then I jumped up and shuffled down the hall, quick and quiet. I had to get to the front door before the bell rang again.

I opened the door, and there was Tara.

"Hi," she said.

I just looked at her. She said, "Are you ... okay?"

"Uh ... yeah." I listened for living-room sounds. Just the TV. No footsteps.

"You said I should stop by," she said.

"I did?"

"Well ... I guess I shouldn't have."

"No! No." I had to act normal. I tried to think what normal was.

"Hey, no, it's great to see you," I said. "How ... um ... how'd you find the house?"

"You're in the phone book," she said, smiling unsurely.

"Yeah, but ..." I looked behind her, for a car or something. There was no car.

Normal, I thought, still listening for footsteps. Act *normal*.

"Hey, come in," I said. "But we have to be kind of quiet. My dad's in the living room. He's ... taking a nap."

Her head cocked a little, probably at the sound of the blaring TV. Neither of us said anything. *Please don't yell right now, Dad*, I pleaded in my mind.

Tara came inside. Before closing the door, I glanced around outside.

"Did you get a ride here?"

"No. I walked."

"You walked? But don't you live up on ..."

"Yes," she said, and her shiny dark hair rippled as she nodded. "I like to walk."

"Oh. Well ... would you like something to drink?"

"Sure. Just water."

Uh oh.

We went into the kitchen and I was reaching for a glass, wondering what I was going to do with it, when footsteps came thudding our way. I looked back; Tara was glancing politely around the kitchen when my dad clumped in. He had the refrigerator open and was reaching into the twelve-pack box when he noticed the girl standing beside him.

He looked her up and down. He looked at her chest. He was breathing loudly through his nose. He smelled from the garage. I wanted to die.

"Who the hell are *you*?" he asked.

Tara's head drew back. She didn't say anything.

"I'd like to know, goddammit," he said, looking from her to me. "I'd like to know what kind of trash my son sneaks in here when I'm not looking."

"Dad!"

"Shut up." He stared at Tara.

"Dad, *please*."

He whirled to me. "Didn't I just say *shut up*? For your information, I'm your father and I need to know what the *hell* is going on here."

I did not know what to do — but, somehow, Tara did. She looked at me, not at him. She looked steadily and calmly at me.

"I guess I'll go now," she said. "Would you walk me out, please, Casey?" She said this in a gentle but firm way, like she was making it clear who would come and who wouldn't.

I followed her out of the kitchen, and stumbled after her to the front door. Tara was the first person who had used that door in months. Gliding to it gracefully, she opened it like it was her door; then she turned back to me and ticked her head toward the outside. I followed her out, and shut the door.

I was totally ashamed. I looked at the ground. She bent down, found my face.

"It's all right," she said. "It's not your fault."

I blinked.

"Listen," she said, "you can call me, okay? We can

talk about the project. I mean, if you want to."

I was still looking down. She was still bent low, looking up into my eyes.

"It's not your fault, okay? Please don't feel bad," she said. "All right?"

I shrugged. "I guess."

She stood up. "Okay then." She stuck her hands in her pockets. Turned to go.

"Wait a second," I said. "How are you getting home?"

She tossed her hair. "I'm walking."

"But ..."

"It's fine — really," she said. "I like to walk. I walk a lot. I'll see you." She was backing up. "All right?"

"Well ... okay."

"All right," she said, and she turned and started walking. I watched her go down the walk, then up the street with long strides. I watched till she was out of sight.

As I came inside and closed the door quietly, I heard the garage door rumble up. I looked out a window to see my dad's car pulling out. He drove off toward town.

He shouldn't be driving, I thought. What if he gets hurt, or arrested? I should have been there. I should have *stopped* him.

It's not your fault. It was like I was hearing her say that again. *But it is*, I thought. He wouldn't get so upset if I just could make everything okay. If I could just ...

No, I thought. *No.* I always think the bad things happen because I'm not trying hard enough. But not this time. Not this time. This was *not* my fault.

Yes it was. It was. I should have seen it coming — I should have asked if we could go to the game right away. Right after the recycling. I should have done that!

No. That's ridiculous.

I could have fixed the faucet myself. Maybe I could have.

That is *totally* ridiculous.

But ...

I didn't know what to think; I just didn't know. Everything was a mess. I didn't want to see or feel what a mess it was. I didn't want to be here. I wanted to take off, like he did. Like he *could.*

I went down the hall, out into the garage.

In the clutter of my dad's workbench, among jars with nails in them and old magazines and a half-repaired fishing reel with dust all over it — with dust all over everything — I pulled out a little wooden box with a sliding top. No dust on that.

I slid open the top. I picked out the rolled-up ziploc bag, the little orange lighter, and the little glass pipe. When I'd tried this once before, I was glad to find the pipe. He had rolling papers in there, too, but I didn't know how to use rolling papers. The pipe was easy.

I unrolled the bag. I reached in and broke off bits from the dry, pale-green stems, very small bits from here and there so my dad wouldn't notice. I crumbled up the bits on top of a magazine. I loaded them into the pipe, and I picked it up. I flicked the lighter. It still worked.

Where could I go? What could I do? I didn't want to be here, not here inside. I was vibrating, everything was vibrating. I didn't want to be here. Where could I go?

I walked out the side door and down the street. I didn't want people to see me. If they saw me they might wonder. I didn't want people looking out and wondering.

The old climbing tree was across the street. Its bushy branches, bright orange and shimmering ... the old tree. Nobody would see me in the old tree!

Oscar and I had these special places, from when we were kids. This was our observation tree, where we'd climb up and look out. And there was the black path — that's what we called it, because it was black asphalt — that went from our school to the train station on the edge of downtown, alongside raised-up railroad tracks.

The path led to our safety spot. That was a shady place under a little bridge where the path crossed a stream. We figured nobody much looked under that bridge — so the space under there was where we'd hang out, on summer days mostly. It was our safety spot.

We were just kids playing around, back then. We'd climb down from the bridge and walk alongside the stream, turning over rocks to find orange newts. They're almost fluorescent, and if you grab fast you can catch them. Later on we'd lie around under the bridge, doing our word games and thinking up adventures. Some of the escapades we'd imagine, with us as heroes of course, would include the safety spot, the black path, and the observation tree.

I started climbing the tree, inside the bright leaves. I climbed up and up, hand over hand, branch over branch — then I got scared. I was up high. Too high. Could I get down? I didn't know how, suddenly. Couldn't remember. Felt scared. Too high.

I climbed down shakily. Confused, I hurried back in my house.

I went into my room and closed the door. Got out my old Legos, dragging out from the closet the blue plastic recycling bin that had them all in it. Dumped Legos on the floor and started building. Then I decided to put on some music.

I went in a drawer that had a bunch of vintage old cassette tapes of kids' music. My parents had found them at a garage sale. My sister used to listen to them, then I got them when she got older.

I found the tape I was looking for. It was one I used to listen to with my dad, after we'd finished reading stories at night. I'd be trying not to fall asleep, trying to keep him there, and I'd ask for this tape. It was one we both liked.

I got out the cassette player. It was dusty but it worked. I couldn't find the power cord but it seemed to have decent batteries. I put the tape on, then built and built with the Legos while it played. After a while I stopped building, and just got lost listening.

At the very end was my favorite song, our favorite song. When the tape would get to it, my dad would switch off the light because this was the last one. We would listen together in the dark. At the end of the song my dad would kiss me goodnight, then he'd get up and softly close the door.

The song is called "Little Brown Dog." While I lay there the tape would keep going, repeating itself automatically. That's when I would fall asleep, while the music kept on playing in the dark.

Oh I buyed myself a little dog
Its color it was brown
I taught him how to whistle,
Sing and dance around
His legs they were fourteen yards long
His ears they were so broad!
Around the world in half a day
Upon him I would ride

Sing, tarry all day
Sing, autumn to May ...

When I woke up it was dark. The tape was still going, but the batteries were dying. The music was all distorted, slowed down and strange.

I sat up, turned on a light. Everything was the same — but it all seemed strange. Distorted and strange. Like nothing was the same.

I went to the kitchen, and looked out the window. My dad's car was still gone. When I turned on the faucet for a drink, there was only a hiss. There was no water, I remembered now — but I was so thirsty. I got some grape juice from the fridge, and drank it from the bottle.

I stood there, leaning against the sink, and it all played back in my mind. The horrible things he'd said, then what she said. *It's not your fault.* I still didn't know about that — but I did know the same tape had been playing, over and over here in our house. The same things had been happening again and again, and they were getting worse.

They were definitely getting worse.

Those things were not going to stop on their own. I suddenly saw it: how everything would just keep getting worse, and worse and worse, until somebody did something to stop the tape.

I went to the phone and called my aunt.

"Hello?" she said.

"Okay."

"Huh? Casey?"

"Yeah. I don't know what it is. But if you think it'll work, I'll do it."

There was a silence.

She said, "Okay."

Part
Two

7.

"Wait'll you see his car," said Julie, rolling her eyes.

"Why? Is it cool?"

"Well ... not *exactly*. Or maybe it is, in a way. You know how they say dogs are like their owners? I think Joe's car is kind of like Joe."

We were back in Ike's, sitting in a booth by a window waiting for this guy. He was the one Julie wanted us to talk to — the one she'd been talking to. I was having a hot-fudge sundae with chocolate ice cream, which Julie thought was weird. But she'd said I could have whatever I liked. This was what I liked.

"He's an interventionist," she said. "I'll let him explain."

"Is that like a therapist? I'm not talking to any therapist."

"He's not a therapist. At all." She was looking out the window. "*There* he is. See the blue car?"

"Which blue car?"

"That one."

I saw it. "That's a *car?*"

She giggled. "That's Joe."

"Whoa."

Out there inching our way in nearly stalled traffic, in a line of small cars and compact SUVs that all pretty much looked alike, was Joe's Cadillac.

This car covered about half an acre. It looked like an old freighter ship. I *guess* it was blue — the color was so faded it looked silver or gray, but then what would it have been to start with? I could see how blue was the best possibility. The door on the driver's side was red, like it had been pulled out of a junkyard and stuck on.

The large-headed guy inside the car had an elbow hanging out his open window. When he saw Julie, he grinned this big spreading grin, and waved this very large hand.

That was my first look at Joe Buffalo.

You might figure a guy who was at least six and a half feet tall, who had a stretched-out head with everything on it exaggerated — wide mouth, long nose, high eyebrows, very large ears — and whose hands were so elongated you'd swear each finger had an extra segment, would eat one of Ike's biggest sundaes in one gigantic bite. But Joe just had coffee.

First he shook my hand, wrapping it up in his. "Hiya, Casey," he said. "Heard about you. Like to hear more." Then he went to get the coffee. He was wearing a brown sport jacket that looked like it came from a thrift shop a long time ago, and some kind of golf shirt. When he'd gone to the counter, Julie raised her eyebrows.

"Don't judge by what you see," she whispered.

I shrugged. Actually I thought he looked ... interesting.

Back with his coffee, Joe bent himself into the booth next to Julie, facing me. He folded his long fingers around his cup.

"Casey, I don't know how much your aunt has told you," he said.

"Not much," Julie said.

He nodded. "That's probably good. Hear it from the horse's mouth." He smiled. Actually, I thought, he did look kind of like ...

"I'm someone who works with families," Joe said, "when they're in a certain type of situation. Any idea what that might be?"

I shrugged. Looked away.

"Yup," he said, nodding — "it's not easy to talk about. Maybe somewhere down inside you know what's going on, but it's never been okay to talk about it. So you never have."

He studied me. "Am I making any sense to you here,

Casey?"

I shrugged.

"Casey," my aunt said. "Can you use your words?"

"I'm not in *preschool*."

"Okay." Her hands went up. "Okay."

"Hey, it's fine," Joe said. "Like I say, this is pretty regular. But my job, I gotta tell you this, Casey, my job is to be very real with people. I mean like ridiculously real. You think I might be suited for that?"

He spread his hands, like a human pterodactyl. I couldn't help it — I laughed. Joe laughed, too. My aunt looked at us, perplexed.

"I think you and me could maybe talk together, Casey," Joe said. "I get that feeling. So. Okay with you if I take a shot?"

He held up his hands, like he was about to shoot a basketball. "One shot at being real. A free throw. Whaddya say?"

I couldn't help it. I liked this guy. I said, "Okay. One."

Joe pretended to spin the shot off, then ducked his head like he was watching it. Now he looked in my eyes.

"It's not you," he said. "You're trying hard. But you're a little bit worried about your dad."

I ... nodded.

Joe clenched his fist: "*Yes*. One for one. Okay if I keep going?"

I shrugged, like I didn't care — but I heard every sound in the room. The wheeze of the door being opened. The clink when a glass got set down. Everything.

"So your dad works. And he comes home from work," Joe said, hands around his coffee. "Take last night, for example. Your dad got home. Stop me if I wander off the factual path here. So far so good?"

I nodded.

"Okay. On the path for now," he said. "So when your dad came home last night, what'd he do?"

"What do you mean?"

"I mean, first thing," Joe said. "Dad's home, you're there. What'd he do first — start making dinner? Rake the leaves, help you with your homework, have a drink? What was the first thing he did?"

"Well ... I guess he had a drink."

"Okay. Sure." Joe nodded. "Lots of people do that at the end of the day. What kind?"

"What kind?"

"Yeah. Kind of drink."

"Well ... you know."

"I don't, actually," Joe said — "but if we're being real here, I'm guessing you do. Can we be that real? Did you notice what he had?"

"Well, you know ... I don't know."

Joe just waited. He sipped his coffee. I saw bottles in

my mind. I was tossing them in the dumpster. Fast as I could.

"A bottle," I said. It's not that I didn't know what it was. It was just ... we never said.

Joe nodded. "Okay. Beer?"

I nodded. Sure.

"And did he have just one? Then make dinner?"

I didn't answer. This wasn't so fun.

"Okay. He didn't have just one." Joe paused. "Did he make dinner?"

"Well, yeah. Pretty much."

My aunt's forehead crinkled. "Pretty much?"

"Well, I mean he started dinner. He always does — and he buys the food," I added.

My aunt was looking perplexed again. Joe glanced at her, then back to me.

"So ... okay," he said. "Math was never my big subject. Actually I never had a big subject. But I'm figuring if there's two of you — that's the total, right? Two. And if one of you starts making dinner but doesn't always finish it, the one who *finishes* making dinner ... I'm just taking a guess here, start with two, subtract the one, carry the seven ... that leaves one. And that would probably be you. Am I right, more or less?"

I smiled, looking at the table. "More or less."

"So where'd your dad go while you were doing that?"

I shrugged. Didn't look at them. "In the garage."

"In the garage? Is he a handyman?"

"No. He just goes out there."

"How come?"

"He just does, okay?"

Joe nodded, settling back. "Okay," he said. "I'm thinking the garage is a tough place for us to be right now. Let's get back to the math. We were doing good with that, right?"

I nodded.

"How many beers you figure your dad drank last night?"

"How many?"

"Yeah. In round numbers. Carry the seven," Joe said.

"Ahm ... I don't know."

"It's okay, Casey." Joe leaned close and dipped his voice low. "You can tell me. I'm a drunk."

"*What?*"

He grinned, sipped his coffee. "Yes sir, that's right. You can't tell me anything your dad's done, said, or drunk that beats the things I've done, said, or drunk myself." He sat back. "Haven't had a drink in sixteen years, and I can't say I remember every one I had. But one day back there I realized I'm an alcoholic. Realized. That word comes from *real*, right?

"Well, so," he said, "an alcoholic is one type of addict. I was a couple of types — alcohol and pain

65

pills. And for a long time I was sort of aware I had this problem — but I didn't *realize* it. Didn't want to face it. Had not said that word out loud."

"Huh."

"The fact is, some people — a lot of people, actually — get to where they can't control their drinking, or smoking or pill-taking or whatever," Joe said. "Sometimes it takes a while for that to happen, sometimes it happens fast. And Casey, this doesn't mean those folks are bad. It means they're hurting inside."

All of a sudden the room went blurry ... and I was leaking. Tears were leaking down my face, I couldn't stop them. Julie offered me a tissue. I didn't want to take it, but then I had to; I could barely see her hand. I swiped at my face, tried to pull it all back. Hold it all in.

"It's okay," Julie said. "It's okay to talk about it."

But I didn't want to. No way.

Joe just waited. Then, he sighed.

"I get it," he said, gently. "I do. You guys have been through a lot. Your parents broke up, what, a year ago?"

I nodded.

"Right," he said — "and none of this is easy, Casey. I know how tough it can be. So if it's okay with you, I'd just like to say some stuff from my own experience. Not just from my life, but from working with people. With families.

"Okay if I do that?" Joe asked. "You don't have to

say anything."

I finally had some control back. I was shaky … but I nodded.

"All right," he said. "So this thing we're talking about, what people call addiction, it lives inside you. It feeds off your body and mind, and it gets stronger and stronger — and meanwhile the real you gets weaker. That's what happens. After a while, to someone who knows you and cares about you, it can seem like you're not the same person any more."

"Yeah!"

"Yeah." Joe nodded. "You know. This is real. And the thing is, Casey: it keeps getting worse. Or it *can*, unless the person who's in this situation faces it and gets some help. And what can make a difference is if some people who really care about this person sit down and are honest with them. If they tell this person the truth — in a caring way.

"That's called an intervention. It's what I do," Joe said. "I work with families and people to help them do this in a planned-out, careful way. If we do it *just right*, we can break through. Sometimes. We can take a shot. Do you get it?"

I did. Actually, I did.

"I think so," I said.

"Okay. So we haven't committed to doing anything — we're just talking," Joe said. "And in talking, it'd be great if I could ask you some questions. Just a few? All right with you?"

"Um ... I don't know."

"Is that a no?"

"Casey," my aunt said. "It's okay to ..."

"I know. It's all right," I said to Joe.

"If you don't like a question, don't answer it," he said. "No problem."

I nodded.

"Okay. Does your dad drink every night?"

I looked at the table. I nodded.

"Does he drink pretty much until he goes to sleep?"

I ... nodded.

"Do you sometimes have to put him to bed, instead of him putting you to bed?"

I looked up. How did *he* know?

"Believe me, Casey, I've been there," he said. "And this is not your fault."

There it was again.

My aunt's eyes bulged. "Casey," she said — "do you think this is *your* fault?"

"It's not like I put him to *bed*," I said to Joe. "He falls asleep. On the couch. I just put a blanket over him, and stuff."

Joe nodded. "Do you never quite know how he'll be? I mean, when he comes home?"

"I don't! Sometimes he'll be happy and act like we're

best friends, then his face'll get all red and he won't talk to me. Or he blows up at something ... or somebody. Sometimes he's okay — sometimes he's just mean. I never know."

"In the morning," Joe said, "does he ever tell you how sorry he is for something bad that happened, and promise he'll never drink or do anything like that again?"

"No," I said. "He never talks about it."

"No matter what?"

"No."

Joe leaned back. "So there it is," he said. "There's the wall."

"The what?"

"The wall. In your house it's never been okay to talk about this. And guess what? We just poked a hole in that wall. It's still there, but we punctured it. We let in a little fresh air."

I didn't say anything. Joe looked at me, and waited. I finally shrugged. "So?"

"Well, so that's it," he said. "We spoke some truth — and there were no explosions. Nobody got scorched, nobody got burned. How does it feel?"

I shrugged. "Okay." But actually, it sort of didn't feel bad.

"At this point," Joe said, leaning in closer, "we'd like to ask you to join our team. We're starting a process that will lead to a small group of people who care about your dad being honest with him in person. We would do this, like I said, in a careful, planned-out way. I'm not saying it'll be easy — but I am saying I know how to do this. And I think we can do it together."

Joe glanced at my aunt. She nodded at me. Joe sat back, and studied me.

"Casey," he said, "if we do this, you would be the key player. If you join our team, we've got a shot. Whaddya say? Can we take it?"

He lifted his hands like he had the ball again, and looked at me. I stared down at my chocolate-on-chocolate sundae. It had almost totally melted.

"I ... guess," I said.

"You'll join us? We can do this?"

"All right. Yes."

Joe made the shooting motion; then he pumped his fist like he'd swished it.

"You and me, Casey," he said. "We are undefeated."

"We didn't *do* anything yet."

"But we did — we spoke the truth," he said. "Out loud. In a situation like this, that's not nothing."

"Huh."

He stuck out his enormous hand, to shake. I shrugged ... but I shook it. My aunt's eyes were shining.

"So," I said. "Now what?"

8.

"Here's the basic plan," Joe said. "One day in the near future, your dad will walk into your living room, and our team will be there.

"Each of you will tell him how you've been affected," he said. "By his drinking. You'll be well-prepared. You'll say what you've seen."

"Will my dad know this is going to happen?"

"No, he won't. If he knew, he wouldn't come."

"So we're going to, like, ambush him? Seriously?"

"You're going to tell him the truth," Joe said, looking at me straight. "Casey, addiction distorts things in a family. If there was a problem, normally you'd talk about it — but in this situation, it's like you and your dad have made a deal *not* to talk about what's really going on. Maybe your mom and your sister made the same deal. Is that possible?"

Take care of your dad, my mom keeps saying. Not

How are you? Just, *Take care of him. He needs you.*

My mom never said how she felt about things, either. When she was here, she just took care of everything. She made things seem okay, mostly. Until she stopped. Now I was supposed to do it, like the job had been passed to me.

It *had* been passed to me.

"Casey?"

"Huh?"

"A lot of families are like this," Joe said. "Believe me. This stuff is everywhere."

He and Julie just sat, and waited. Waited ... for me. To say something.

I did try.

"I ... you know ... I don't know," I said. "I guess I always thought ..."

I frowned at the brown goo in my dish.

"What?" Joe said. "That no one else would understand?"

I looked up. "Yeah."

"Sure. You think you've got to keep everything inside the family. And that's a pattern — it gets passed down. Kids grow up feeling like they should never trust other people — like nobody *would* understand. They start having problems in their own lives. And it goes on and on.

"An intervention breaks that pattern," he said,

"because you're straight. You come from the heart." He tapped his chest. "That changes things. You and I, we've seen a bit of that change right here. Don't you think?"

"But ... what about my mom? Will she be there?"

Joe looked at Julie.

"We don't think she should," Julie said.

"Why not?" But I knew why not.

"We just ... don't know if she's ready to face this," she said. "She's very protective."

"So who *would* be there?"

Julie told me. Oscar's dad, from down the street — he's known my dad as long as I've known Oscar. A lady my dad works with, Ms. Jacobs, who I don't know. My dad's doctor. Julie. Joe. Me.

It hit me how few friends my dad had left.

"We think hearing the truth from you will be most important of all," Julie was saying. "You mean the world to your dad, Casey. It may not always seem that way, but it's true."

"We're not saying it's safe for any kid to come out and tell the bald truth to an addicted parent," Joe put in. "That could be dangerous. That's why we'll plan and prepare so carefully — to make this not just real, but safe."

"Okay," I said. "When?"

"Soon," Julie said. "We've planned it for next Tuesday, a week from today. I've already approached the other people. They can come."

"We'll have one goal," Joe said. "To get your dad into treatment that day. That afternoon."

"Treatment?"

"Yes. It's a special hospital, Casey — here in New Hampshire, just an hour away. It's one of the best places he could go. They'll be ready for him. We'll finish the intervention by asking your dad to go directly to this place for help."

"I'll be ready to take him," Julie said.

"How long would he have to stay?"

"Maybe a couple of weeks," Joe said. "Up to a month."

"A *month?*"

"You could stay with me," Julie said quickly. "We'd visit him every week. Every day, if you want to."

I looked at them both. This was a lot.

I said, "Will this work?"

Julie took a breath, and turned to Joe. He leaned over the table again.

"It doesn't *always* work," he said. "I'll never lie to you, Casey — addiction is tough. It doesn't want to come out into the open. But we'll do our best to do this right, so your dad can see how things are — and how he can get better."

I was looking at the table. I was a thirteen-year-old kid, you know? This was a lot.

"I've done this almost a hundred times, Casey," Joe said softly. "I know how to do it."

Julie was looking back and forth between us. "And it does work sometimes," she said. "Right?"

"Oh yes," Joe said. "This is our best shot. It can work."

Again, they were waiting. For me.

I said, "Okay. Tuesday."

"At four p.m.," Julie said quickly. "We'd like to be ready at your house when your dad comes home from work."

I said, "Comes home ..." I looked up at the clock. It was almost five.

"Oh my god — I've gotta go! My dad'll be *home*. I haven't picked up or anything. I've got to go!"

Julie stood up. "I'll take you," she said.

In Julie's car my mind was scritch-scratching around like an unhappy hamster. *What'll he say when he walks into his own house and these people are waiting for him? What'll he do?*

"My dad's going to kill me," I said.

"No, he isn't," she said. "We'll explain that we had ice cream together. No mention of Joe or what we talked about. Okay?"

I took a deep breath. Let out a sigh.

"What?" she asked.

"Well, I mean ... you guys just said we're going to be real, tell him the truth — and now we're getting ready to lie to him. I mean right? And we'll be like lying to him right up till we spring this whole thing on him. We'll be planning it all behind his back. I mean we will, right?"

For a minute Julie just drove. Then she said, "David is so defensive right now. If we let him know what we're doing before we do it, he'll wall us out. Totally. You know how he can be."

I didn't answer.

"Anyway, it's not *lying*, Casey — we really were having ice cream. We just have to keep this very, very quiet between us right now. It's delicate and difficult and we've got to do it right. Can you see that?"

I wasn't sure. It was starting to rain. Water was spattering the windshield. Suddenly it wasn't so easy to see.

"This won't be easy," I said. "Will it?"

"No," she said. "But it's really, really important."

"Yeah." I let out one heavy breath.

"Day after tomorrow, Thursday," she said, "we'll meet again after school. Same place, same time. Okay?"

"Okay, but I can't take so long."

"We won't. I promise."

We were pulling into the driveway. It was raining hard.

* * *

Julie went through the garage, opened the inside door, and stepped into the house. I followed, holding myself tight inside.

But the kitchen lights were on brightly. The room was filled with cooking smells, and with a simmering sound. My dad was at the stove, his back to us. Julie marched in.

"Hello, David," she said. "I've brought your boy home."

I hung back, just inside the doorway. My dad turned; but he didn't look angry.

"Is that where he was. Hey, Caboose!"

"Hey," I said, edging in. "I'm sorry I didn't get to do the, um ..."

But the breakfast dishes were not in the sink. They'd been done. The kitchen looked clean.

"We had some ice cream," Julie was saying. "I've seen so little of Casey, I thought it'd be fun to hang out a little. But I guess we overstayed. I hope we didn't ..."

I went into the living room. It was picked up. The beer bottles from last night were gone. The blanket and pillow were gone from the couch. It was all straightened up. Even the window shades were lifted up partway. I went into the bathroom and, very quietly, turned the water on just a little. A trickle came out, then a stream.

He must have called a plumber. The bathroom was clean, too. Maybe my dad came home from work early, to meet the plumber — and that's when he cleaned up. I knew my dad wouldn't explain. But that's what must have happened.

And now he was cooking dinner. There was no beer bottle on the counter. And his eyes didn't have the funny, backed-away look from the garage.

"I'm glad you had a chance to hang out," he said to Julie, talking politely like she was someone he didn't know that well. He leaned against the counter, arms folded across his chest.

"Thank you for bringing him home," he said.

He didn't offer her a drink or anything. He just nodded at her, like he was waiting for her to leave.

"So, David," she said. "How is everything?"

"Oh, fine," he said. "Busy, but not bad." He turned back to the stove, to his cooking.

"Have you ... how's work?"

"Just fine."

"Have you talked to Shannon?"

"Not lately," he said without turning around.

"David ..."

"What?"

My aunt sighed. "Nothing," she said. She peered out the window. "I guess I'll sail off. Literally."

Out there the rain was driving down hard. This would have been a good night to ask her to stay for dinner. My aunt. His sister.

"Be careful out there," my dad said, still not turning from the stove.

"Oh ... I'll be fine," Julie said. She turned to me. "I'll see you, Casey. Okay?"

"Okay."

And then she was gone.

We had steak and crinkly freezer fries from the oven, and salad. While we were eating my dad said, "You know, ah, Casey ..." He cleared his throat, and stopped eating. He was looking at his food.

"I know I've been kind of erratic lately," he said, "and unfortunately, I guess you've had to carry the load. More than you should have to. I want you to know that's going to change."

I looked at him.

He looked up. "Okay?" he said.

"Uh ... yeah. Okay."

"Okay." He looked back down, and cut into his steak.

My dad didn't have a single beer or go into the garage at all that night. I realized how I knew from little sounds and smells just what he did, and when. Like I had some kind of antenna up, always fine-tuned. I never realized that before.

But that night he didn't do any of it. None.

Maybe it *was* going to be different.

Later, he came in and helped me with my homework. Other times when I needed help he'd come in all bleary and weird and lecture me, or he'd get impatient and frustrated. Once when I had a math problem I couldn't get, he blew up. "A damn *fourth grader* ought to know this crap!" he said, and stomped out.

But tonight he helped me with some math and he was patient and cheerful. After he left, I had to write down some brainstorming for social studies about *Johnny Tremain*, that book I'd finally started about Boston before the Revolution. When my dad came back in at bedtime, I told him about it. He started talking about the Freedom Trail. He said it's in Boston — it visits the historic places from back then.

"We'll go do it," he said. "You and me."

"We will?"

"Sure. Soon. I wish I'd known about this report — we could have gone last weekend."

Last weekend?

"Anyway, we'll go," he said. "Just us. Soon."

"That'd be great, Dad."

"Okay." He turned off the light. "Good night, son."

"Night, Dad."

And he shut the door. I heard him walk to the living room and turn on the TV.

* * *

I lay there in the dark. I couldn't sleep. After a long time, I switched on the light. I got up and looked at the *365 Days of Total Trivia* calendar on my desk. Did you know Istanbul, Turkey is the only city in the world that's on two continents? I did not know that.

Yes, and this intervention thing was going to happen next Tuesday. That was less than seven days away. Joe said if we did it, if it worked, things would be different.

But things were already different. They had been tonight, and my dad said they'd be different. He said so.

Now what?

9.

The next day I got permission to go see Mrs. Suboski, the guidance counselor. You don't have to say why you want to see her, you just have to go there if you say you're going there.

I opened her door a crack. "Come in, Casey," she said from inside.

Mrs. Suboski's office is a narrow room, no windows, with posters all over the walls. "Don't Let Your Life Go Up In Smoke." "Everybody Is Somebody. Nobody Isn't Anybody." "Got Problems? Tell a Counselor." "You're People Not Sheeple." That last one I didn't totally get.

Mrs. Suboski herself looks like an amphibian. Her head is round and she has blinking eyes magnified by large squarish glasses. She smiles at you a lot. She smiled at me now.

"Please — have a seat," she said brightly.

I sat down in front of her desk. She brought her

chair around and sat down, a little too close to me.

"Something I can help with?"

She had this orange rug thing on the floor. I stared at it.

"Is it about school? Or more about home?"

"It's ... more about home."

"Whatever it is, Casey, anything you say will be just between us."

I looked up. "It's kind of ... about my dad."

She nodded.

I told her some of it.

I told her my dad was drinking beer a lot. I didn't mention the garage. I told her it was just him and me. I didn't say how I was finishing cooking dinner, or cleaning up when my dad got sick. I told her about Julie and Joe, and next Tuesday.

She nodded. When I was done, we were both quiet for a while.

"They want you to be part of this intervention," she finally said. "Yes?"

"Yeah. They say I'm really important, because I'm like ... the kid."

"You are," Mrs. Suboski said thoughtfully. "You know, it seems like a lot to put on a kid."

I nodded. "Yeah."

"How do you feel about that?"

"I don't know."

"What about your mom and Shannon?" She remembered the Medalist. Of course.

"Well, they're in Maine. They live there now."

"Couldn't they come?"

"I guess, but ... Julie and Joe don't think they'd be ready for it."

"Mm-*hmm*. Are you ready for it?"

"I don't know. I thought I was, I thought it might work. But last night my dad said things were going to be different — and then he didn't drink at all. So now I don't know what to do."

Mrs. Suboski nodded again.

"What I hear," she said, "is that you are a twelve-year-old boy — is it twelve?"

"Thirteen."

"A thirteen-year-old boy trying to make a life alone with your dad, and you've been placed in a very difficult situation. Does it feel that way for you?"

"Well ... sort of."

"It's not that interventions can't work — they sometimes do," she said. "But they are confrontational. They can lead to ruptures."

I looked up quick. "What do you mean, *ruptures?*"

"I mean you and your dad are important to each other right now," she said. "An angry break on his part, and you'd be ... well." She folded her hands.

"It's not my role to tell you what to do," she said.

"But I can point to alternatives. If your dad says things are going to be different, you *could* consider giving him that chance."

"Yeah, but ... I told them I'd do this."

"Yes, and you can go ahead with it, if you decide to. But it *is* your choice, Casey. If you choose not to cooperate, they can still do it, can't they?"

"I don't know. I'm not sure."

"Well, what I'm hearing is that your connection with your father is very important in your life right now," Mrs. Suboski said. "I'm just wondering if you want to try doing something that might place that in jeopardy. You don't know how your dad would react. He might be very ..."

"Defensive?"

"Yes. He could be."

"My aunt said he's defensive. But they said we'll tell the truth, only, like ... from the heart."

I was embarrassed. Mrs. Suboski just nodded.

"Yes. Well. I'm certainly not saying you can't do that. But I also appreciate that you've been put in a tough spot. I just hope you'll think about your options. You can come talk with me about it anytime. Okay?"

I just looked at her.

"It's your decision, Casey," she said. "It's not your aunt's decision, or this interventionist's decision, well-meaning though they may be. What you'll choose to do is up to you. And there's a lot at stake here."

She stood up. She smiled at me kind of drearily. Then she looked at the clock.

"Why, it's seventh-grade lunch period. I'm sure you're hungry — and you've only got fifteen minutes. Will you come talk again, if you need to?"

"Oh, sure."

Mrs. Suboski patted my shoulder on the way out.

In the hall I saw Tara coming. She spotted me. I'd been avoiding her all week; I was still intensely embarrassed about what happened at my house.

"Hi," she said, coming up. She glanced at the counselor's door, and her forehead wrinkled.

"Are you ... okay?"

"Sure. Why wouldn't I be?"

"Well ..."

"No, I'm sorry," I said. "Really, things are fine. Are we going to work on the project?"

"Um ... I hope so," she said.

"Okay. I'll call you."

But I wasn't going to call her, I was going to avoid her. She'd seen too much.

She brightened. "Are you going to lunch?"

"No! I have to go ... to my locker."

I turned away and hurried up the hall. I could feel how red my face was. That had been completely lame and awkward. I was hungry, and as I walked I thought, *My locker?* There was no food in there. But I couldn't go to the cafeteria now. She'd be there.

I could go to the library. I'd hang out there till lunch was over. Then ... well, then I'd have to starve the rest of the day.

When school ended I saw Oscar up the hall, opening his locker. As I came up, he eyed me warily.

"Hey," I said, looking into his locker. "What d'you have to eat?"

"Um ... why?"

"Because I'm gonna die if I don't eat something. I didn't get lunch."

He shut the locker door. Crossed his arms.

"Why should I feed you?"

"Be ... cause we're friends?"

"Yeah? So how come you've been acting like a percolating turd?"

"Um ... I don't think a turd percolates."

Oscar grinned. "A permutating turd," he said.

"A perambulating turd," I said, and I made a walking motion with my fingers. "Strolling around school."

"There's a few of those," he said. "I'm looking at one now."

"All right, okay," I said. "I'm *sorry*."

"No you're not. You're hungry."

"I'm hungry *and* sorry. I'm sorrgry. It's a serious condition."

"But rarely fatal," Oscar said. "Unfortunately."

He opened his locker. Rooted around inside.

"Most of what I got's pretty old," he said. "Would you prefer something with fur or without?

"Ugh." I looked over his shoulder. "Like what?"

He reached into his upper shelf. With a flourish he pulled out two long, red floppy things.

"Red licorice!" I said. "Acceptable."

"Oh. Imagine my relief." He handed me one, then reached in the locker for his hat.

We picked up our backpacks and walked out the front door, chewing together. I knew I didn't have to rush home and clean things up, because my dad hadn't left a mess. Things felt different. Things *were* different.

"You want to go downtown?" I said. "Mess around a little?"

He grinned, and clapped on his hat. "Thought you'd never ask," he said.

The sun was glancing through clouds and the air was cool. It was a nice fall afternoon. We walked along crunching through fallen leaves.

"Hey," I said, shoving my hands in my pockets. "Sorry if I've been, like, erratic lately."

"Er*rat*ic? Hey, good word, frecklehead. Where'd you

get it?"

My face got hot. "I don't know."

"Anyway, you haven't been erratic, you've been a dork. Weirdly antisocial. But what do I know — maybe you needed to be home cleaning. Keeping everything lemony-fresh."

"It wasn't about *cleaning*."

"Oh, good. I was gettin' worried about waxy buildup."

"Waxy *buildup*?"

"You know — on your floors," he said. "When you clean too much. Big concern."

He lifted his hand, gazed at it.

"*I Was a Teenage Housekeeper*," he said. "By Squeaky Clean."

"Squeaky is not a name."

"There was a crazy lady one time that shot the President," he said. "*Her* name was Squeaky."

"It was not."

"Swear to god! I *know* my weird-name history."

"Okay, so what about Oscar?"

"Hey, don't be makin' fun of *my* name." He spread one hand proudly on his chest. "I was named for Oscar Peterson, the great jazz pianist."

"Dude! You said pianist!"

We kicked leaves at each other, sauntering along. We jumped up to grab branches, swinging and dropping

89

into people's neatly raked piles. It was like old times.

Now we were walking past stores, eating candy bars.

"Let's play blind man," Oscar said.

"Oh, no. No. We're not cute kids any more, Oscar."

"We're still cute, man!" He pulled a pair of
sunglasses out of his backpack. "At least, I am." He put
on the shades. "Come on."

"Aw, *man* ..." But I followed him. I did use to like
this ridiculous game.

"This one?" I asked, passing the greeting-card store.

"Naw. That lady's got no sense of humor," Oscar
said.

The liquor store. "*This* one?"

He grinned. "Not yet."

He stopped before Old World Paints.

"Coach Marconi's in here," he said.

We had Coach Marconi in Little League. He's a
good guy. "He doesn't deserve this," I said.

"What? It's live entertainment. No charge," Oscar
said. "Gimme your arm."

A bell jingled as I pushed open the paint store's door.
I was holding Oscar by the elbow, guiding him in. With
his free hand he felt the door, felt my face, felt the air.
A couple of people turned to look. Behind the counter,
Coach Marconi, a big man with a soft round face that
smiled easily, saw us and rolled his eyes.

Oscar started murmuring, feeling around. "Oh mah god. *Oh* mah god. Where am I?" In his black hat and black shades, he looked like an old blind bluesman. "Where *am* I? Oh mah god."

There was a pyramid of paint cans on the floor. Oscar veered toward it while I held onto his elbow from behind. His free arm was out ahead, feeling his way.

"Emmeline? Where are you, Emmeline? I'm here, honey! I'm comin', Emmeline!" I was trying not to laugh. He'd never talked in Blind Man before.

Oscar lurched toward the can pyramid, his hand out groping. A woman nearby rushed over to stop him before he stumbled into the cans, which of course he wasn't really going to do — but when she grabbed his arm, she stumbled backward just enough to bump the pyramid.

The whole thing rumbled and teetered. Coach came rushing around the counter, and Oscar whirled around the lady to grab the top cans. He steadied them just before they would have fallen, to total disaster. The woman put her hands on her hips.

"Why," she said, "you can see as well as I can."

Oscar stopped. He slowly looked around.

"My god," he said. "I *can!*"

He took off his glasses. "I can see! It's a *miracle!*"

Coach, shaking his head, went back behind the counter and reached down. He came up with one of those wooden paint stirrers.

"Hold him steady," he said to me. "Maybe take off that hat."

"Whoa," Oscar said, "not the hat! Let's go, Elmore!"

He grabbed my arm with one hand, clamped the other on his hat and scuttled us out the door. We started up the sidewalk, and ran straight into Oscar's dad.

"Whoa," he said, hands out to stop us. Mr. Terry squinted at his son, who'd put his shades back on. Then he broke into a broad grin.

"Let me guess, now," Mr. Terry said. "The Other Blues Brother?"

"He's the Master of Disaster," I said.

"Grand Master Flush!" Oscar said, one finger in the air. Then he glanced back at the store. "And we kind of need to go."

"Oh my. What *have* you done now?" his dad said in his excellent accent. "Or is it best not to ask?"

Oliver Terry, Oscar's dad, is from the Caribbean — from Grenada, which is an island down there, and he talks in this looping, swooping, musical way. He's a nice man, and he has a great smile. He was smiling now, though also shaking his head.

"We were doing street theater," Oscar said. "Great art is not always appreciated right away."

His dad nodded. "Do I need to stall any pursuers?"

"That might be good," Oscar said. "See you tonight!" — and he took off.

"Chicken pepperpot!" his dad shouted after him.

I sighed. At Oscar's house they had incredible dinners, like every night. His dad was the cook.

"See you, Mr. T," I said, and I took off after my friend.

Now we were running up the sidewalk, dodging people and letting out pent-up laughter till we could hardly breathe.

Oscar bent over, chest heaving. "Did you *see* that lady's face? 'Why, you can see as well as *I* can!'"

"Yeah, but, dude. You really have to call me Elmore?"

He looked at me, eyebrows raised, hands on his knees. "If we're gonna do street theater," he said, "you have to be a character."

"I think you have that handled."

"I didn't say you're the *main* character."

"Whatever," I said. "Race you to the path."

"Aw, come on man, I'm portly!"

But I took off running up the sidewalk.

"Hey, stop that boy!" Oscar yelled at the started passers-by. "Stop him! He's having fun!"

The black path runs along the outside of our downtown.

Like I said before, it goes from our school, alongside train tracks raised up on gravel, to the railroad station at the edge of downtown. A lot of people who take the train to work use the path. In the woods it crosses this short little bridge over a stream. Under the bridge was our place. Our safety spot.

We stopped on the bridge and tossed pebbles down at the stream. Then we saw a few people walking this way, probably from the station.

"Intruders," Oscar said. "Possibly alien."

He went to the end of the bridge and swung himself over the guardrail. I followed. We went scrambling down the steep bank of dark, sharp-edged shale.

In the shade and the sloping bank beneath the bridge, some blue Bud Light cans had been tossed around, messing up our space. The empty twelve-pack carton was shoved up where the underside of the bridge met the gravel bank. We pulled the carton free, then crouched around tossing cans into it. We stopped moving when we heard the people's voices coming closer on the path.

We stopped and were silent. It felt cool to hear the footsteps and the conversation move slowly overhead, from one side to another, when the grownups walking and talking up there had no idea we were down here.

When the sounds were gone, we started chunking pebbles into the stream again.

"So," Oscar said. "What's going on?"

"What d'you mean?"

He leaned over to get a stone, and tossed it. It hit the water with a *plunk*.

"Well," he said, "every day you've been rushing home to take care of stuff. So what's up with your dad? Doesn't he take care of stuff?"

"Well ... he's sort of having a rough time."

"Like since your mom took off?"

"Yeah. Especially since then."

Oscar nodded. "My dad's worried about him."

"Really? He said that?"

"Yeah. Your dad's like out of touch. My dad doesn't see him or hear from him any more."

We both looked at the trickling water. Finally I said, "I guess I figured if I made everything okay at home, then he'd be okay too."

"Huh. Well ... did it work?"

"No."

"So, I mean, is this why your folks broke up?"

"I ... don't know. My mom used to take care of everything — she made things *seem* all right, you know? But I don't think they really were. Now she's just obsessed with my sister."

"Your *sister's* the one going to have problems, man," Oscar said.

"Seriously? Shannon?"

"Come on, she's driven like a fire truck. Clang, clang, *whooeee!* 'Everybody look at me! Everybody clap now!' What's going to happen when everybody stops clapping?"

"Huh. So, what — I'm the lucky one?"

"Yeah, man." Oscar chuckled, and waved at our shady space. "You got the safety spot."

We looked around for good throwing stones. Oscar found a nice flat, smooth-edged one. When he skipped it, it glanced off the water and hit three different wet stones before finally plopping in the stream.

"Whoa," he said. "You see that?"

We were walking up the path, on our way home.

Oscar said, "You think your dad's depressed?"

"I don't know. Maybe that's part of it."

He looked at me. "Just part?"

"Well ... I don't know."

We walked along. Oscar said, "It's okay to talk about it. I won't tell anyone."

"Well ... I guess he's kind of got a problem."

"You mean with drinking?"

I stopped dead. "Where'd you get that?"

He shrugged. "My dad mentioned it. It's what he's worried about."

I started walking again. Oscar caught up.

"It's okay, man," he said. "I mean, it's not *your*

fault."

I walked faster. "Why does everybody say that?"

"What d'you mean?" He was scuttling to keep up. "Who else said it?"

"I've been talking to some people," I said. "There's this thing we're supposed to do."

"What thing? Will you slow *down*, man?"

I did. We'd come to the avenue across from school. Cars were rushing by in both directions.

"Okay," he said, puffing. "What's this thing?"

"My Aunt Julie started it. It's this planned-out thing where we surprise my dad when he comes home from work, and we tell him what he's doing with the drinking. How he's messing up his life and stuff. Julie talked to your dad about being in it. They say I need to be in it, too."

"Huh. You gonna do it?"

"I don't know. Should I?"

"Well ..."

Oscar stood up and shoved his hands in his pockets. Cars whizzed past.

"If your dad's not doing that great," he said, "and if there's something you can do that might help him get better, then you need to do that thing. I mean right? He's your dad."

We stood there a while.

"But this isn't kid stuff," I finally said. "It's not a

game."

"So? Anyway you're terrible at games. I have to do everything."

I laughed, a little. We watched the traffic. Then I remembered something.

"I saw a t-shirt on this lady the other day," I said. "Know what it said?"

"*I desire Casey Butterfield?*"

"Oh right. No, it said, *Just call me Cleopatra, Queen of Denial.*'"

"Uh ... Hey, I get it! Queen of the Nile. Like in Egypt."

"Oh, you're quick."

"So, is this a title?"

"I think so. I think my dad's like the king."

"Yeah? Of denial?"

"Kind of like."

"So that's it," he said. "That's why you need to do this thing."

"Yeah, maybe, but ... what does that make me? I pick up his bottles, I clean up after him — I'm like his servant sometimes. Am I the serf of denial?"

"No, man — you're the prince," he said. "The prince of denial. Unless you do something about it, you inherit the title."

"Huh." I thought about it. "That's what Joe said."

"Joe?"

"Oh, man, you got to *meet* this guy. He's the one directing this thing we're supposed to do. Hey, are we gonna cross or what?"

Up the avenue is a stoplight, with a crosswalk and a button you push when you want to get across. You weren't supposed to cross anywhere else. Before and after school there were monitors at the crosswalk, to make sure.

Oscar looked up the avenue. The light up there was turning red. Cars were slowing down. In the other direction, cars were just starting to come up from downtown.

He clamped a hand on his hat. "Let's do this!"

We ran across like renegades. Sometimes you have to break a rule or two.

10.

That night my dad had a beer at dinner. But he cooked dinner again, and he was quiet and nice. He always used to be nice, really to everybody.

But something wasn't the same.

When we were eating our hamburgers and cheesy noodles, I asked, "How was work today, Dad?"

"It was okay."

"Anything special happen?"

"Not really."

"I've got to write an essay tonight. Well, a rough draft."

"Hmm."

"It's for this project about old Boston. Remember, the Sons of Liberty and stuff? I'm supposed to describe an idea for taking a different look at something that happened then. You know, like that the colonists should have boycotted that tea instead of dumping it all in the harbor. You see?"

"Sure. You better get to it. Right after dinner."

"Well, the problem is I'm not sure I *have* a good idea."

"Uh huh. Well, you can do it," he said.

And that was that. My dad ate quickly. Instead of more beer, he had brought home a tub of vanilla ice cream. I thought we'd have it together, but when he was done with dinner he scooped himself a big dish and carried it into the living room. I heard the TV come on.

I sat there for a minute. Then I started cleaning up, so I could go work on my essay.

A while later I went into the living room. This was different — I hardly ever went in there nowadays, after he'd started watching TV. It was like this was his territory.

He was watching some noisy news show about Hollywood celebrities. I thought it was stupid, talking about actors like they're world leaders. Or maybe they are, I don't know.

"Dad," I said from behind the couch.

"Uh?"

"Those guys. You know, the revolutionaries in Boston?"

I came around to the side of the couch. He was still staring at the show.

"Uh ... yeah. Sure."

"We talked about them. Last night."

"Uh ..." He looked at me. "Yeah! I know."

"Well, I was wondering. Did those guys actually fight in the Revolutionary War, or did they just stir everybody else up until it started? I mean, you never hear about Sam Adams fighting in an actual battle. Or John Hancock. Maybe they did, though, I don't know. But I thought it might be a different point of view, saying how they started this whole war, then they stood back and let other guys get killed. What do you think?"

He'd already turned back to the TV.

"Yeah." His head bobbed. "That'd be good."

"But what do you *think*, Dad? Is it a good point, or is it, you know, stupid?"

"Of course it's not stupid. You're smart."

"But ... how would I research something like that?"

He gave a quick sigh. "*I* don't know ... Google it. Don't you have a book on the Revolution?"

"Yeah. We used to read it."

"Right. Start there."

He turned and looked at me. "You can do this, Casey. You're smart." And he turned back to the TV.

"Yeah," I said. "Okay."

When I left the room, the TV was talking about doing a big explosion for an action movie. How cool that was.

11.

"He only had one beer," I said, next day at Ike's. "But he was weird."

"In what way?" Julie asked.

"I don't know, like he didn't want to deal with things. Like he wanted to just watch TV and eat ice cream."

"I hate to tell you, Casey," Joe said, "but that's kind of typical. An alcoholic'll try to cut back, their intentions are good — but until they face the whole deal, sooner or later this thing is going to climb right back in the driver's seat."

I was having a small, plain dish of chocolate. I was getting tired of ice cream; I was here so Joe and Julie could tell me what I was supposed to do. It was Thursday. The intervention was five days away.

"You call it 'this thing,'" Julie said to him — "but what *is* it? Help us understand. Say more."

"Well, I'm not much of a theory guy," Joe said as he twirled the stirrer in his coffee, "but I think it gets to be like there's two minds inside the same person. One mind is the addiction — that's totally focused on protecting itself and getting what it wants. It's selfish, only wants its buzz. That's the side of your dad you don't understand right now," he said to me.

I said, "You think he has two *brains?*"

Joe grinned. "That sounds weird, right? But I do think the addict's mind becomes divided. There's the guy you know and love, and then there's the addiction — which, like I said before, is a powerful adversary. It's got an arsenal of tricks and disguises, camouflages and bombs to throw ... everything. We can't fight it head-on."

"We can't?"

"No. It's like trying to battle a fog, or a shape-shifter. That's why we'll do the intervention when he hasn't had a drink yet that day. Then we can speak to the original person. *That* can work."

Julie said, "How?"

"You speak from the heart, and you speak the truth," Joe said to both of us. "Honesty helps you reach the real person. Speaking with love helps him face the truth."

He looked at me. "That's it. That's the formula."

"So it's simple," said Julie.

"Well, not *easy* — but simple, yes. One message, one

goal. Go into treatment. Today. That first step is always the biggest one."

"Was it for you?" I asked.

"For me?"

"Yeah. You said you're an alcoholic, right?"

My aunt said, "Casey ..."

"No, it's fine," Joe said. "You want to hear my story? Really?"

"Yeah," I said. "I do."

He drank some coffee. "Okay."

Joe swirled the stirrer, which was tiny in his giant fingers.

"I was an ordinary guy," he said. "Still am, you know? I got through college okay, down in Providence — Bs and Cs, but I made it through. I didn't get into dope and I didn't drink very much, though I had plenty of friends who did. I played a lot of ping-pong." He grinned. "I'm a *wicked* ping-pong player. And I had a good time. I'm not saying I never partied ... I just didn't do too much of it.

"After college I started teaching shop in a city high school. I really wanted to work with my hands, maybe start my own business — but this was a decent job and I could do it, so I did. I went along that way for five or six years. Then I had my accident."

He held up his left hand and turned it over, palm up. A thick, gnarled, whitish scar ran on a ragged angle all the way up the palm. It looked like he'd cut his hand in half.

"My god," Julie said.

"I was running the table saw, in the shop at school," Joe said. "Ever see a table-saw blade — how big it is? Well, a couple of kids were screwing around and they bumped me from behind. I fell toward the blade and my hand went out. It just ... happened."

"What did it feel like?"

"It *didn't* feel, at first. I just looked at it. My whole hand was sliced open like a bunch of spareribs. It was just ... I don't know. Then I passed out."

Joe shook his head.

"In five months I had four operations. I was in and out of the hospital; my doctors weren't sure if I'd be able to use my hand again. I had to do six hours of therapy and exercise, six *hours*, every single day. It was a workplace accident, so I was at home on disability. I was bored, depressed, and in serious pain every single day for months. Every exercise hurt. The hand hurt all the time; sometimes I couldn't sleep, it hurt so much. The doctors gave me narcotics — Percocet, then OxyContin — trying to mask the pain. I took them. I mean, my doctors told me to.

"The pain pills made me feel okay or even good for an hour or two, then I'd be even more depressed," Joe said. "So at night I started drinking, just for a break.

Just to feel *different*. It got so I was blurred out all day on the pills, then stewed in alcohol from six o'clock on. Then five o'clock. Then four.

"I was so bored, and so *lonely* ... no work, just endless exercises and pain I didn't want to feel. Trying not to feel the pain was the main thing. It was taking over my life."

Joe shrugged. "I think that's what it's about, really — addiction, I mean. It's about manufacturing different feelings, good feelings, so you don't have to feel what's really there. But the problem is, the good feelings you can manufacture aren't that good, they don't really last, and after a while they aren't even feelings. You just get numb. You're desperate not to feel everything that's backed up inside you, and by then you're totally disconnected. From yourself and from everyone else.

"That was the worst thing — being so alone," Joe said. "When I'd see my friends I'd put up this front, all cracking jokes and sociable, then I'd get away soon as I could to go home and get high. Or I'd arrive high, and if people were drinking I'd pound it down.

"All the time I thought nobody noticed. I thought I was hiding it *so* well. It seemed incredibly important that nobody should find out what was really going on, what I was really doing. I just wanted to stay home, by myself, watch the tube and try to get another buzz. For three years that was my life. Three *years*. Can you imagine?

"I'd call doctors all over the city, and out in the suburbs," Joe said. "I'd say I was in town on business and I had this severe hand injury and I'd run out of my pills. Could they help me out? Sometimes I'd even drive out to the western part of the state, call docs out there. If a doc was skeptical or suspicious, I'd go to their office and show them my hand. That always took care of it.

"Then one spring my friends Jerry and Simone from college, they were married and they had a house outside Boston ... they insisted I come for Easter dinner. Said they had a bunch of our old friends coming. Well, it was true, they did. Only they weren't coming for Easter. They were coming for me.

"They told me to get there in the morning, 'cause we were going to eat at noon, right? But when I got there, they were all waiting in the living room. Jerry introduced this woman who said she was a nurse and a recovering alcoholic. This woman said, 'Joe, these people are all here because they love you and they're concerned about what's happening to you. These are your friends. Will you sit down and hear what they have to say?'

"I went cold inside," Joe said, "but I sat. And they didn't tear me to pieces or tell me I was the gruesome loser I secretly thought I was. They just told me what they'd seen, and how it had made them feel. I couldn't believe how much they *had* seen! Basically they said I wasn't me any more. They said they wanted me back."

Joe paused, and stared at his coffee.

"What happened?" I asked.

"Well, that was it. At first I got mad, then I got embarrassed, then I was ashamed — and finally I started to realize what it meant. I mean, I had convinced myself these pills and drinks were my real friends, the ones I could rely on. But here were my *actual* friends, and they were telling me the truth. I couldn't believe it. But, at the same time ... I could.

"I basically went limp. It was like I finally, finally relaxed. They said they had a place for me at this hospital, the one where you'll ask your dad to go. They had everything all set for me to go. So, I just ... I basically just said okay."

Joe paused. He looked down.

"I stayed in that hospital a month," he said. His mouth squeezed tight. "I felt a lot of pain. The physical pain was back — and now I had emotional pain, too. It wasn't a picnic. But to *feel* it ... that was like a liberation, you know? I mean, these were real feelings, and it turned out they weren't nearly as awful as the nightmare prison I'd trapped myself in.

"And I made good friends at that place. We got through things together. I had my old friends again, too.

"That was sixteen years ago," Joe said. "I've been working for the hospital the last twelve. I travel all over New York and New England in my old car. I get to work with people like you, Casey, who want to do for someone they love what my friends did for me — offer them the chance to get clean and come back to life. That's what it's all about.

"So now, that's what my life is all about."

We were quiet a minute. Ike's jazzy music percolated in the background. Finally I asked, "How's your hand?"

"Aw, it works pretty good," Joe said, flexing his extra-long fingers. "Not as good as if the accident never happened, but ... accidents happen to everyone, one way or another. Things we never planned on. Things that hurt. Like a family breaking up, for instance. It's a weird thing to say, but what I figured out is, you have to go right through what hurts. You've got to live right through it."

He turned his hand over. "If you do, then one day you get to the other side."

He made a fist, then opened it.

"So that's what happened to me."

"We'll go over the ground rules next time we meet, on Monday after school," Joe said. "Right now, the most important thing is for you to write what you're going to say to your dad."

"*Write* it? Can't I just say it?"

"You think you can, but you don't know how

you'll feel in that moment," Joe said. "This'll be a tense situation, Casey. I want everyone to write what they'll say, rehearse it, then bring that script on Tuesday. You will read *exactly* what you wrote.

"Everyone will take their turn saying their piece to your dad," Joe went on. "We'll plan and practice who goes first, who goes next, even where people will sit."

"When will I go?"

"I'll get to that. But tonight, when you write this ..."

"I have to do it *tonight?*"

"Yeah," he said. "If you put it off, you'll just get anxious."

I was already anxious.

"I want you to write like you're talking to your dad — because you will be," Joe said. "First, you need to tell him you love him. Say why."

"I have to *say* that?"

"You don't have to use the word 'love' if you're not comfortable with it — but what are the things you appreciate most, in your relationship with your dad?"

"Well ... I guess the way we used to spend time together. Do things."

"Right. Great. Write specifically about a couple of those things," Joe said. "Say why they mattered to you. Then tell him what's changed. I want you to describe one particular incident when your dad's drinking affected you in some major way. The details you remember are what'll tend to really connect.

"So," he said. "When I ask about a specific incident, does anything jump into your mind?"

He and Julie looked at me. I didn't answer.

But of course, something did.

Here's what I wrote that night, sitting at my computer.

I really did the best I could. Googled stuff and ran spell-check, so I'd get the details right.

Dad,

When I was little you'd take me to the playground, and we would play baseball games that I'd always win. I think you let me win, right? Well I liked it anyway. A lot. And I remember the first time you took me to Fenway Park. It was just us, and I remember how I held your hand going up the ramp and then I saw that field for the first time, that incredible grass. We saw that together, remember?

But it wasn't just big trips, it was also how we'd read together every night. If you were away and mom came in to read, it wasn't the same. When you did it, I'd lean my head against your chest. You might of thought I was sleepy but I loved how the words sounded, coming up in you.

You don't come in to read any more dad. I know I'm older, but you stopped coming in a while ago. And now even if we wanted to, you couldn't. Most nights you're too messed up. I hope you won't hate me for saying this dad but I feel like you're going away somewhere. We're in the same house, but it's like you're going away.

I kept on making excuses for it, like the ones mom made. You were tired. You were sick. You were upset. But since mom and Shannon left it's been me taking care of you, dad. I put a pillow under your head on the couch, I bring a blanket to put over you. I finish cooking the dinner, and I clean up after. And I been rushing home from school to pick up the beer bottles in the living room. I kept on trying to make things nice so when you got home you wouldn't get upset. But it really didn't work dad. You said things would change, but dad I don't know.

And I have to say this thing about what happened last Saturday. I'm sorry but I have to say it. You said we were going to go watch football at the college, but then we didn't. You got too messed up, and then this new friend of mine came over, a 7th grade girl. She just wanted to talk about a school project, but you came in and called her a piece of trash. A piece of trash dad! I almost threw up I felt so bad.

Sometimes you throw up, and you leave it for me to clean up. Sometimes you don't come home and I don't know where you are. And I know what you do in the garage, dad. I ...

* * *

I backed up and erased that last part, about the garage. I knew I couldn't say that, not out loud. I didn't know how I could say any of these things — but they were true. I had never said or written them before. But there they were. Right there on the screen. They were true.

I looked for a few long minutes. Then I hit Save.

That night my dad brought home a six-pack. Not a twelve-pack, and not two six-packs. Just one. And he only took ice cream into the living room after dinner. But later, I heard him come back into the kitchen, and I heard the refrigerator door open and close. I heard the bottles clinking as he lifted out the six-pack, then took it with him into the living room.

12.

Friday at the end of school I saw Tara in the hall. Except for that one time, I'd avoided her all week. I hadn't called her about the project, even though I'd said I would. When she saw me now, she held her books tight against her chest and kept on walking.

I came up to her locker.

"Um ... hey," I said.

"Hello." She was putting books in her backpack, not looking at me.

"I guess I haven't been, you know, too friendly this week," I said.

"Not too."

"I know. I ... still want to do the project. I mean, if you do. It's just that, you know ..."

She turned to face me. Her eyes were brown and soft.

"What?"

"Well ... I guess I was embarrassed. It was *terrible* what happened at my house. It makes me sick to think you saw that."

"I know but ... it's okay," she said. "I kind of understand."

"Really? I don't see how."

"You don't have to." She picked up her backpack, closed her locker door. We started walking.

Now I really wanted to make things okay. "Anyway," I said, "that's why I didn't call or anything."

She nodded. "But here you are."

"Yeah. It's been a big week."

"It has? And I missed it?"

I laughed, a little. "Yeah, well next week's going to be even bigger. Hey, listen." This just popped out. "You want to do something tomorrow?"

She nodded. "Okay. What?"

"I don't know." And I didn't. "Maybe ... there's a football game."

She actually giggled. "A football game? Us?"

"Well, why not? At the high school. It's fun. Ever see one in person?"

"I've never even seen one on TV. Should I come to your house?"

"No! I'll meet you downtown," I said. "How about Ike's? No, wait. The bagel place."

"The one near the supermarket? What's it called?"

"I think it's called The Bagel Place."

"Oh! Well, yes. That's fine."

"How about if we meet at noon?" I said. "The game starts at one."

"That's fine too," she said.

About six that night my dad called. I could hear noise in the background, people talking loud.

"Listen, Case, can you get your own dinner? I'm tied up a while."

He was at a bar, I knew it. This happened a lot on Friday nights. I remembered last Friday night, at the Jefferson Inn.

"Dad," I said. "Don't, okay?"

"What?"

"Just please don't. Okay?"

He didn't say anything. I could hear other people talking and laughing.

"Dad?"

"I don't know what you're talking about, Casey," he said quietly, warningly.

"Dad, you said it would be different. You said I wouldn't have to, like ... carry the load."

"I'm asking you to get your damn *dinner*. For *once*. You think you could step up, think you could man up and do that? One time?"

I wanted to say, *But it's not one time. It's never one*

time. But I didn't.

"Sure. Fine."

"All right. *Thank* you."

The phone disconnected. I sat there, looking at it in my hand.

When Saturday morning came I left at 10:30. My dad wasn't up yet, which was no surprise. I didn't want to be there when he got up. He'd be in a crappy mood.

So I wrote a note and put it on the kitchen counter, saying I'd gone to the game at the high school. I hadn't asked permission, but I figured, Why would he care? It felt really nice that I was heading out to do something with Tara.

I slipped out the garage side door. It was overcast outside, a light gray day. I had a jacket on, but it wasn't really cold. I needed to do something to waste a little time before meeting her, so I walked by the school and along the black path to the library.

These days at the library, I had a choice — go downstairs to the kids' floor, or straight ahead to the adult part. The YA books were downstairs, but that still felt like the kids' area. So I went straight ahead. I read *Sports Illustrated* and *ESPN the Magazine* until it was time.

The bagel place really was called The Bagel Place. Tara was already in there, sitting at an empty table.

"Hi," I said.

"Hi!" When she smiled, her face lost all its shadows.

Then I realized I only had four dollars. I wanted to be able to buy a couple of sodas, at least, at the game. I didn't have enough to get something here, too. *Nice thinking ahead,* I thought.

"Uh ... we probably ought to walk right over there," I said. "Get good seats."

"All right."

She was wearing a dark red jacket. It was simple and old-fashioned. Sort of different-looking.

"Um ... that's a nice coat," I said as we walked.

"Oh, thanks. It's boiled wool."

"Really? People boil wool?"

"I guess they do. It came from Austria."

"I never heard of that," I said. "Boiling wool, I mean. I've heard of Austria."

"It was my mother's," she said, and as she looked down she blushed.

"Oh god," I said. "I'm sorry."

"About what?"

"I don't know — I said something. You're upset."

"No. It's not you."

"Uh ... well ..."

I was confused. She just kept walking. As I kept up, I said, "Don't let me mess things up again, okay? When I start messing things up, just stop me. Okay?"

"All right," she said, with her hands deep in her jacket pockets. "But ... if something's kind of messed up and it's not your fault, can I let you know about that, too?"

"Oh, yeah. Sure."

"All right," she said — but that was all. We didn't talk any more. Which, at that point, was fine with me.

Our high school and my old elementary school are around the corner from each other, and behind them is a big parking lot that they share. The football field is back of that, surrounded by a chain-link fence with bleachers inside. On this side of the fence, the elementary-school playground is sort of stuck in between the football field, the parking lot, and the back of the grade school.

As we came up the driveway, we could see cars filling the lot, and a bunch of people crowding around the gate and ticket booth. Inside the stadium, over where the running track curves around the end zone, our band was milling around in their blue-and-white uniforms. Beyond them, an ambulance was parked on the grass.

The stands were filling up. Grownups and teenagers were walking on the track, standing around in clumps, or getting sodas and hot dogs at the snack shed. On the grass by the ambulance, little kids were playing football and racing around.

"Pretty big crowd," I said.

"Is this an important game?"

"Who knows?"

Tara pointed to the playground, to the slides and stuff. "Let's go there," she said. "Just for a minute. Want to?"

"Sure."

So we did. While everybody else filed through the gate and found seats in the bleachers, we slid down the slide. We rose and fell and laughed on the seesaw. We pushed the puke-a-whirl (that's what Oscar and I called the little merry-go-round thing), and when it was going good we hopped on and looked at each other. Tara's hair floated out behind her as the world rotated past.

When we got dizzy on the puke-a-whirl, we climbed up on the jungle gym. We sat perched up on top, watching the people. Then we started to talk. And we forgot about the people.

We talked about friends we'd had, about things we did when we were younger. We talked about shows on Nickelodeon and the Cartoon Network, the ones we'd liked and the ones that were stupid. We disagreed about the sliming on Nickelodeon, which I thought was hilarious and she thought was ... well, not. We talked about music and books and weird experiences. Tara had only come to New Hampshire two years ago, from Minnesota, which she said had even longer and colder winters than ours, if you could imagine that. I said I wasn't sure I wanted to imagine that.

She said in Minneapolis you could walk for miles through these tubes that connected the buildings, so you could be warm and dry and you didn't have to go outside in the wintertime. I *could* imagine that. We talked about zoos we'd gone to, pets our families had had. I had an aquarium full of little red-ear turtles once; she had three guinea pigs and two cats. We didn't talk about the people in our families at all.

From the stadium we heard the brassy clatter of the bands, and looked up to see the teams running out. First came the other guys, in red and gold — then there was a stomping roar and our players' blue helmets came out, bobbing over the people along the sideline.

After the game started, we kept hearing the crowd noise surge from one set of bleachers to the other, depending on who did what. The announcer's voice floated back and forth. "Ball is carried by number thirty-one ... Mackenzie ... three yards ... tackled by Boyd and Christopher ..."

"Want to go in?" I asked.

She was swinging her legs, holding the bars we were sitting on. "I like this," she said.

"Yeah."

"We can go in if you want to."

"Nah. Not yet."

"Okay!"

She swung down inside the igloo of connected rods. I did the same thing. We sat on the ground inside there a long time, and just kept talking. The sounds of the game washed over us and we talked. We were still sitting in there, talking, when the announcer's voice drifted in and stopped us.

"Will Casey Butterfield please go to the first-aid station? Casey Butterfield, please report to the first-aid station."

13.

Tara's eyes went wide. Heat came into my face.

"That's you," she said.

"Yeah."

"But why?"

"I don't know." I didn't — but I had a bad feeling.

"You stay here," I said. "I'll come back."

"No. I'll come with you."

I didn't argue; I wanted her to come. As we rushed toward the gate, she took my hand. My face felt warm for two reasons, now.

The man at the gate held out his hand to stop us.

"They called my name on the loudspeaker," I said. "I have to go to the first-aid station."

"Oh. Okay," he said, letting us through. "Head for the ambulance," he called after us — "beyond that end zone."

It was halftime; people had come down from the

stands and were everywhere. We plunged into the crowd, holding hands tightly as I led the way, threading past the lines of people at the snack shed.

That's when I saw my dad.

He was stalking back and forth in front of the ambulance, jerking red-faced on stiff legs. There was a pool of space around him in the crowd, like people were keeping their distance. The first-aid guys in their jumpsuits sat on folding chairs by the ambulance, not looking at him. To anyone else, I'm sure he looked angry. But I could see he was drunk.

Tara's grip tightened. But I let go.

"Stay here," I said.

"No. I'll ..."

"No! No way. *Stay* there."

I started to move toward the ambulance and my dad spotted me. He lunged ahead and tore into the crowd, actually shoving a few people out of the way. I stood frozen. He grabbed my arm hard and stuck his face in mine.

"You are in *serious* goddamn trouble, young man," he sputtered at me. His eyes were slits. He'd been in the garage, too. "Now *move!*"

He yelled it so loud people around us jumped. He pitched forward, and yanked me after him so hard I stumbled into a couple of high school guys, who put their hands out. "*Whoa* — easy, man," they said, but I was already getting jerked past them, like a bad dog on a leash.

He didn't say a word, just kept this grip clamped on my arm as he stomped forward and hauled me along. People were jumping out of the way, everyone turning to look: high school kids, little kids staring with wide eyes, kids my age whispering and giggling, grownups drawing back with faces like masks.

Tara was gone. Everything was gone. I was stumbling, stunned, seeing the faces in flashes and trying to keep my balance after every angry jerk on my arm. I tried to say something, but nothing came out. I couldn't make words. I didn't know any words except "Dad ... *please*," and those I couldn't say.

He pulled me through the gate. The man who had let us in looked at me now with sorrowful eyes. Nobody had stopped us. Nobody the whole time stepped up to say, "Is this your kid, mister? Mister, what the hell are you doing?" Nobody.

He opened the back door of his car, grabbed my jacket and my belt, and heaved me in. I bounced off the seat, my head smacking into the back-door armrest. I curled up and lay there, eyes shut tight, arms over my pulsating head.

He got in and sat down with a heavy wheeze of springs, slamming his door. "Goddamn last time *you* go *any*where without asking *me*," he was muttering. "See who the hell is boss around *here*."

There was more under-his-breath cursing until I couldn't tell what he was saying, and didn't want to hear. I covered my ears with my arms.

"This will *never* happen again!" he roared. "Do you UNDERSTAND me?"

I didn't answer, didn't look. Just clenched more tightly. Waited for the blow. The first time my father would hit me. Ever. I waited for it.

He didn't. I could hear him breathing, a dry raspy sound. My heart was pounding so loud.

The key clicked in the ignition and the engine roared. We slammed backward, then lurched ahead. The back end skittered loose as he sped out of the parking lot.

God, don't let some little kid step out from between the cars, I prayed as I lay there. *Please God, don't let my dad kill some little kid. Please don't let him. Please.*

As the car hurtled home and I lay there with eyes squeezed shut, in my mind I saw Joe. We were roaring along the road and suddenly there was his Cadillac, parked right there. As we were just about to pass, Joe opened his door and stepped out, tall and rumpled and real like he was. He held up one gigantic, scarred hand, and our car just stopped. Joe was going to open the back

127

door, Joe knew I was hiding in here ... Joe was going to reach in and protect me and tell my dad the truth about what he was doing. It would be okay because Joe was here.

Then the vision popped like a bubble, and Joe was gone.

We pulled into the garage. The crowd way back there, all those people who saw us, they were gone. Tara was gone. She'd seen the craziness twice, and I knew she was gone. Anybody would be. Now it was only him and me. I guessed that was how it would be, how it had to be from now on.

I was thinking in a clear, calm, strange way, lying there curled up on the back seat. I guessed everybody would be scared of him now, and sorry for me. They would avoid us. They might talk about us, but nobody would talk *to* us. We would be like outcasts.

He didn't say anything. He parked, switched off the engine, got out, and slammed the car door. He pounded up the steps, then the door to the inside clicked open and smacked shut. I heard him stomp down the hall.

I lay there for a long time. I was numb, I guess, or in shock or something. Finally I rolled onto my back and looked at the roof of the car.

I looked at the yellowed plastic light up there that wasn't on, at the dimpled vinyl ceiling that was dirty.

I just looked at it, like when you're sick and almost delirious and you stare at the wallpaper pattern on the wall until the pattern starts to move. After a while I pushed open the door, and crawled out.

As quietly as I could, I went into the house.

My dad was in the living room. I went into my room. I pulled down the shades till it was dim in here, like a dungeon. No outside view, no daylight.

I sat on my bed. My head was on my hands, I was looking at the floor. I heard him come down the hall.

My door opened, and I looked up to see him. He was breathing heavily, wheezing a little. He had a beer in his hand.

"You left without permission," he said, murkily. "You left a little note, like that did it. That did not do it. From now on you will not leave this house without asking for and obtaining my permission, do you understand me? Not even to take out the garbage, which you *will* do.

"I'm sick and tired of your crap," he said. "You think you can do whatever the hell you want? Well you can't. Not anymore you can't. You will not go out, you will not have your sneaky little friends over. You *will* do your chores and your homework, and you will do nothing else without first getting my goddamn permission. If I feel like *giving* my permission. Do I make myself clear?"

I just sat. Didn't look up. Didn't answer.

"Do I make myself *CLEAR*?"

I nodded.

"*Say* it."

"Yes," I murmured.

"Louder."

"*Yes.*"

"You will not leave this house without my permission?"

"No."

"You will do your damn chores?"

"Yes."

"Right. That's all I have to say to you."

He turned and shut the door. I just sat there. Nothing was going through my mind.

Nothing at all.

That was a dark afternoon.

I curled up on my side, on my bed. My dad had turned the TV on loud in the living room. Football. Once in a while I heard footsteps go into the kitchen, at first thumping and angry, then later shuffling and out of it. After a while, there were no more footsteps. I knew he was asleep. The TV still blared.

I sat up, finally, not wanting to. I looked around my room. There was a lot of crappy kid stuff in here. A Simpsons poster. A Red Sox team poster my dad got for me out of the *Boston Globe* one year. A plastic bank shaped like a football helmet, New England Patriots. A poster of a blue Corvette. It was all stupid crap.

I got up and twisted open the plastic plug on the bottom of the helmet bank. Poured out the money on my dresser. A bunch of pennies, a few nickels and dimes. Worthless crap. I knocked the stupid bank off the dresser; it hit the floor with a smack, and as it clattered off, a last penny rolled out. It fell over and lay there.

Then I slowly, steadily ripped down the Red Sox poster. Two pieces of it stayed on the wall, pushpins holding the torn corners. I crumpled up the poster and threw it in the trash.

Then I took it back out of the trash.

Slowly, steadily, carefully I tore that poster into tiny little pieces. I let them go, let them drift to the floor. Then I sat back down on the bed. To hell with him. To hell with everything.

I sat there for the longest time, for hours and hours, in the room where I had once been a child.

Part Three

14.

It was dark outside. I was still sitting on the bed. I heard a knock on the window. I let up the shade, and there was Oscar.

He motioned for me to pull up the window. I didn't do it. He put his hands on his hips, cocked his head, spread his hands out wide and shrugged — like, *Well?*

I opened the window. About three inches.

Oscar rolled his eyes, then bent his head down sideways to the opening. I figured he'd say something stupid, to be funny. But he didn't.

"Hey," he said.

"Uh."

"Rough day."

So he knew.

"Uh," I said. "So everybody knows."

"Hey, it's just something that happened." He was

still bent down sideways. "It's over."

"No it isn't."

"Yes it is, man. Now open this window, okay?"

"Why?"

"So I can talk to you without deforming my neck for the rest of my life. Okay?"

I shrugged, and pulled up the window. Oscar grabbed the sill to pull himself in.

"No. You can't," I said.

"Not *this* again."

"Yeah. And you have to talk really quiet, okay? He's sleeping."

Oscar did the finger quotes. "You mean 'sleeping'?"

"No. I mean sleeping. And he says I can never have anybody over. Or anything."

"You can never have any*thing* over? Whoa. That does let me out."

He put his arms out like Frankenstein's monster, and staggered around in the dark.

"*The Thing that Couldn't Come In,*" he moaned.

I had to smile. "You are *such* a buffoon."

Oscar lifted his hat, smiled, and bowed.

"How'd you find out about it?" I asked.

He looked to one side out there. Then he stepped aside. And there was Tara.

She stood in the dark with hands clasped, looking

unsurely at me. "I called him," she said. "I know he's your friend, I've seen you together. I ..."

She shook her head. "I had to do *some*thing. I thought about it all day."

There they were. Two people I'd never seen together. Never even thought of together. There they were.

"I'm sorry about what happened," Tara said. "I know how you feel."

"Nobody knows how I feel."

"Well ... I might. In a way."

I looked at her.

"Why?"

Tara stared at the ground. Then she turned to Oscar. "You're not going to do that Frankenstein thing again, are you? 'Cause this is serious."

Oscar spread his hand on his heart, like he was deeply hurt. "I *can* be serious." He looked at me. "Can't I?"

I shrugged. "Anything is possible," I said. "Especially today."

We both looked at Tara. She didn't look back. After a while, she said, "It was my mom."

15.

Tara leaned in through my window. Oscar squeezed in beside her. He'd actually taken off his hat.

"She was like the heart of the party," Tara began. "My parents had a lot of parties — for my dad's business friends, for my parents' regular friends, for charity. My mom had to put on this big show all the time. My dad would come home from work, and then a lot of nights after a while these people would come, too. Lots of people. There'd be music and noisiness downstairs. Our mom would send us to bed, but we'd sneak back down and spy on them. Everybody would be talking loud and having drinks and laughing, and my mom would be in the middle of it.

"She was really pretty. She was tall and dark-haired, and she wore these beautiful, sort of slinky dresses — and everyone wanted to be with her, all these noisy party people. But I don't know if that was where *she* wanted

138

to be. It was fine for my dad, he's a noisy person himself. When he's home, you always know where he is, because you can hear him. But my mom ... I mean, she tried. She would talk and laugh with everyone, and I think she did like the attention. She was so beautiful. But when it was only us, just her and my brother and me, she was really quiet.

"I think she was shy," she said. "Even though she was beautiful, I don't think she had confidence. What she really liked was to go down in the basement and build model airplanes."

"Model *air*planes?"

"Yes, isn't that funny? But not the regular plastic ones. My mom would order these incredibly complex balsa-wood models of old-fashioned planes. She liked the ones the first women pilots flew. She'd tell us about these women, about their planes."

Tara smiled, remembering.

"She made the *Winnie Mae*. That was Amelia Earhart's Lockheed Vega, the red one she flew across the Atlantic Ocean. She also made the Lockheed Electra, the silver one Amelia Earhart disappeared with in the Pacific Ocean, trying to fly around the world.

"She built a model of this early monoplane that a lady named Harriet Quimby flew. Harriet Quimby wore a purple flying suit. She was very beautiful also, and she became the first woman to fly across the English

Channel. Her plane didn't have any brakes. Five or six guys had to hold the plane back while Harriet Quimby got ready in it. Then they'd let it go. That's how she took off."

"How did she stop?" Oscar asked.

Tara cocked her head. "I don't know! She made it, though. Across the Channel I mean. She also wrote Hollywood movies, a bunch of them, back when they were all silent. But she died pretty young, in an accident in a flying show. Her plane stalled out — nobody knows what went wrong. Airplanes had open cockpits back then. She fell out. The people at the air show watched her fall. Like all the way down."

"Whoa," I said.

"Yow," said Oscar. "No *seat*belts?"

"I don't know. I guess not."

Tara paused a moment, looking someplace we couldn't see.

"We've still got my mom's planes in the basement. You'd think my dad built them, but he never touched them. He thought they were beautiful, though. They *are* beautiful — all shiny red and yellow and metallic colors, with exactly the right marks and struts and propellors. I go down there and clean them, really carefully. Then I just sit and look at them."

In the other room, the TV laughed. Part of me kept listening for footsteps from there. But none came. He was out.

"When I look at them, I wonder about those planes
— what they really meant to her," Tara said. "Did she
want to fly and explore, like those women did? Or did
she just want to be alone and quiet? Building those
planes takes a *lot* of time by yourself. You have to be
really, really careful. Mostly my mom worked on them
after we were in bed. When she didn't have to play
hostess, or sometimes after the parties were over, she'd
go down there with her coffee and work on her planes.
She said it calmed her nerves.

"I think my mom was having trouble with her nerves
for a long time, but nobody really noticed," Tara said.
"It's funny, because everyone wanted to be with her and
see her, but nobody really *looked* at her. Everyone told
her she was great because she was attractive. And I think
my mom wanted to believe it — but she also wanted to
be downstairs by herself. Or maybe she wanted to be up
in the sky. I don't really know.

"She did love us, though," Tara said. "She loved my
brother and me. I know she did."

"Sure she did," Oscar said. "Absolutely."

"Everyone drank at the parties," Tara continued.
"And my mom would get sort of wired from the
pressure of being hostess all the time, and I think from
the attention she got — so afterward she'd stay up super
late downstairs drinking coffee. She'd pour liquor into

her coffee. She didn't want anyone to know she was doing that, but I saw her do it a couple of times. She wasn't getting much sleep, and in the daytime she'd be more and more ragged. She still pulled herself together for the parties, though.

"They got a lady to come live with us, to help with my brother and me. That's when we started seeing less of our mom. She'd be in the basement, working and drinking. Coffee and liquor all day long. Finally she had to go to the hospital, because she got so skinny and wild-haired. It didn't really seem like her anymore.

"My dad stopped having parties at our house. I think the doctors told him to. When my mom came home, she had pills to calm her anxiety. She started spending a lot of time in her room, kind of blurred out on those pills. After a while she started drinking again, too. She was hiding bottles in her room. She was in there all the time. She didn't work on her models at all any more.

"Mrs. Grover was taking care of my brother and me, and we'd get to see our mom, like, once or twice a day. She'd be lying there on her bed and her room would be so dim, the shades all pulled down. We'd go in, and she'd give us a kiss and listen to us for a while. But it was like she was a ghost, or a shadow or something. I never understood what happened to *her*."

"What about your dad?" I asked. "Didn't he do anything?"

"I think he tried. But he was so involved in his work, and sometimes he wouldn't come home for a week or something because he traveled. Then it'd be just Mrs. Grover, my brother, and me in the house, and our mom in her room. A couple of times they had to put her back in the hospital, but then she'd come out and be back in her room all day. I guess she sent out for the liquor. I don't really know. She could basically buy whatever she wanted.

"The thing is, nobody ever *talked* about it," Tara said. "Dad and Mrs. Grover would tell us, 'Your mom isn't feeling well today,' or 'Your mom is sick, so she's back in the hospital for a few days.' Or 'Your mom is sleeping right now. She's tired.' As if it was *normal* to be 'tired' or 'sick' or 'not feeling well today' *every* day, and never ever explain what was really going on."

Tara was quiet.

"What happened?" Oscar asked softly.

Tara shrugged. "She died. Right there in her room. They said she took an overdose of alcohol and anti-anxiety medication. They said it was an accident, like you might fall off your bike. You know, 'What a terrible, unexpected *accident*.' And nobody has ever explained anything. I'm not even sure what really happened. *Did* she take an overdose? Did she mean to? Or did she just wear herself down with all that stuff till she died?

"My dad still never talks about it. He's always off on his business now, working late and traveling, and my older brother is stoned all the time and my dad has no idea. And people think I'm grown up or something because I look like my mom and I spend most of my time by myself, because I don't have that much in common with the other ... kids."

She backed out of the window and stood up straight. Out there in the dark, her arms were folded tight across her chest.

"Sorry," I said.

Tara shrugged.

"I wish I could talk to her," she finally said. "I wish I could *tell* her. I wish it wasn't too late."

Oscar caught my eye, and raised his eyebrows. I knew what he meant. It wasn't too late for everyone.

"I better go," Tara said.

"It's pretty dark," Oscar said. "Why don't I get my dad to drive you home?"

She thought about it. Then she said, "All right."

She and Oscar started to go, but she turned back.

"Call me tomorrow," she said to me.

"Should I?"

"*Should* you," Oscar said, opening both palms dramatically. "Like you two don't have anything to *talk* about."

As they started off, Tara turned back again and smiled. It was the kind of shy, bright smile a person might remember for a long time.

16.

Sunday was like a bad wound my dad and I were trying to pretend wasn't there.

Did you ever wipe out really bad on your bike as a kid? You didn't want to look at it, right? I mean, there'd be dirt, gravel, and caked blood all stuck together with pieces of your ripped-up jeans on top of what really hurt; and you dreaded going inside to start cleaning up, because you knew it'd sting wickedly — and that was just when you pulled off the mess on the surface so you could see how bad things were underneath. You just wished the whole slow, sliding crash hadn't happened. So for a while you limped around trying to pretend it never did.

That's how it was.

We didn't talk. We'd pass each other in the house and there would be silence. My dad looked thirsty. Parched. His face was pale, his lips were dry. His eyes had a look of ... I don't know. Confusion, maybe. Or pain.

I knew he knew what had happened. Maybe he woke up in the middle of the night and remembered, because I did: the looks on those people's faces as they stepped out of our way, his fingers biting into my arm, him yanking me so hard my shoulder still ached.

Part of me wanted to say, "I'm sorry, Dad, I shouldn't have done whatever I did to make you so angry, I'm really sorry" — but that was an old part of me. I was *not* going to apologize. All I did was go with a friend to a football game — to a kids' playground, actually. I didn't flip out in front of a stadium full of people. I didn't haul my own kid off like a bad dog in front of everybody. I did not do that, and I couldn't make anything better by pretending I had.

It was like we were on opposite sides of some canyon, across this gulf that echoed with the things we couldn't say. I guess we were afraid to fall in and keep falling. We'd pass each other in the hall and in the kitchen, a few inches and a canyon apart.

My dad's mouth was open, but he didn't say anything. I wanted to hear he was sorry. I needed to hear something. But all day there were no words.

I called Tara.

"How are you?" she asked.

"I'm okay. I don't think my dad is though."

She was quiet.

"I don't think he is either," she said.

"That was fun yesterday," I said. "I mean, before."

"Yes. It really was."

"Thanks for coming last night. Thanks for calling Oscar, too."

"I found him on Facebook, actually. It's lucky he's got an unusual first name. I didn't know his last name at all, but I searched through the Oscars and found him."

"You're on Facebook?"

"Yes!" She laughed. "I have like four friends. You could be number five, if you want."

"I'm not allowed on Facebook. I don't have a cell, either."

"Why not?"

"My dad says I'm too young — but I've started thinking he doesn't want much information getting out. Hey, is Oscar weird or what?"

"He's funny. And he's nice."

"Did his dad bring you home?"

"Yes. He's nice, too — and very funny. I see where Oscar gets it."

"Yeah."

"Does he ever take off that hat?"

"His dad?"

"No, you geek! Oscar."

"Well, only in school. And to shower. I hope."

She giggled. "Hey, we need to talk about the Revolutionary project. It's due a week from tomorrow."

"Oh yeah. That. Actually, I might have an idea."

"Really? What is it?"

"Let's talk after social studies tomorrow, okay? I have to finish the essay tonight." It was going to be almost like a vacation, thinking about history instead of the mess of my life.

"Well ... take care of yourself," Tara said.

"Right. See you."

We hung up. Then I sat there, just looking at the phone.

Take care of my*self*?

Like how?

Julie called later. She got my dad. I picked up the phone in the kitchen; he was on the other phone, in the living room. I could hear the TV.

"How are you, David?"

"All right. Fine."

"Really?"

"Sure. Why shouldn't I be?"

"I don't know. How about Casey?"

"He's fine," my dad said. "He's not here, though."

I looked at the phone. I'm not?

"Oh," Julie said. "Well ... okay. Take care of yourself, okay, David?"

"I guess I better," my dad said, sounding sarcastic. They hung up.

Why would he lie to her? Maybe he just wanted me under his thumb. Or he didn't want any true stories leaking out.

I called Julie back. This was actually fine. He wouldn't know.

"He said you weren't there," she said, sounding puzzled.

"I know," I said. "I heard."

"Huh. Well, who knows? Can you meet us tomorrow after school? One last time."

Holy crap, I thought — the *intervention*. That was on Tuesday — in two days. I'd stopped thinking about it almost completely. It was like that stuff with Julie and Joe was from a TV show I had stopped watching.

"Well ... I guess so."

"Great," she said. "Meet you at three-thirty. At Ike's."

"No."

"Pardon?"

"Not Ike's," I said.

"But that's where we're going to meet. That's where Joe's coming."

"I'm not going there any more," I said. "I'm sick of that place."

"Oh. Well ..."

"You know The Bagel Place? It's right up the street."

"Ah ... yes, I think so."

"If you want to talk to me, that's where I'll be."

There was a long silence. Finally, my aunt said, "Is everything all right?"

I thought, *What a ridiculous question.* But I said, "I'm just tired of ice cream."

"Okay, sure. I'll bring Joe over there. He only drinks coffee anyway. See you tomorrow!"

She hung up. I went into my room and sat there thinking. I could, I realized, go wherever I wanted after school, because I wouldn't be rushing home. I would do the chores my dad said I had to do, and no more. No more. Things were different now.

Let him take care of himself. I wasn't going to be his cook and cleaner-upper and excuse-maker. Not any more.

That crap was over.

17.

Tara waited for me in the hall when we were coming out of social studies Monday morning.

"I saw you handed in your essay," she said.

"Oh yeah. I wrote about how that guy who got everybody in Boston all whipped up to take on the king never fought in any actual battles."

"Which guy?"

"The revolutionary. Sam Adams. That they named the beer after."

"Oh. Well ... maybe he was too old to fight."

"He wasn't too old to stir the whole thing up, was he? He made speeches and led all these meetings," I said. "In Boston he was this big hero. But I read his Wikipedia bio and some other stuff I found — and after the war started, old Sam Adams didn't do much but go to more meetings and talk. I think he let other guys go out and get shot."

Kids were stepping around us in the between-classes tide. Tara gave me a funny look.

"Well, you definitely took a different point of view," she said.

"Yeah. I got an idea for the final project, too."

"Really?" She stopped at an open classroom door. "I have to go in here," she said. But she waited.

"Okay," I said, "picture this. When everyone comes into social studies, there are these unusual-looking crates on the floor. Old-fashioned wood boxes, right? With no explanation. And we're supposed to be there to make our presentation, only we're not. Nothing happens at all — and just when they're about to send down to the office and say we're missing, the door blasts open and we rush in with hatchets. We chop the crates open and dump the stuff that's inside — something dark and dry — all over the floor!"

Tara's mouth was open.

"The Boston Tea Party," I said. "Get it?"

She swallowed. "I was thinking we could make a diorama."

"But this'd be great! *Every*body would remember our project."

"Oh, yes — they'd remember us, too," she said. "'What happened to those two kids who got expelled for bringing hatchets into social studies class?'"

"Well ... I haven't worked out all the details yet."

She smiled, and shook her head as she backed into class.

"We better talk more about this," she said.

Oh sure, I said to myself as I went down the hall to math. *Everybody wants to talk.*

Mrs. Suboski, the guidance counselor, wanted to talk too. I'd gotten a note from her today. "I wonder how you're doing with that project we talked about," she'd written. I crumpled the note up and threw it away.

"Well, we've been *working,*" Julie said in The Bagel Place that afternoon. She gave Joe a satisfied glance. He arched his eyebrows at me. I frowned and looked down.

"Something wrong, Casey?" my aunt asked.

"No."

"Well ... okay. Now, listen, we've done a *lot* of planning and organizing. We've left you out of most of that because you're in the middle of the situation with your dad. We don't want to make him suspicious. But tomorrow, Casey, you'll really be the key person in this."

Inside I cringed. It was like they'd been playing this game they thought was so great. But where were they when the real trouble happened?

I knew that didn't make sense, but I couldn't help it. They weren't there on Saturday — and after this intervention escapade made a whole new mess of my life, they wouldn't be there, either.

But I would.

I was having a sesame bagel with plain cream cheese. I kept stirring my hot chocolate, making little circles with the wooden stirrer while Julie talked. Joe was leaning back, watching me.

"We have a place all set for your father at Chestnut Ridge — that's the treatment center," Julie said. "Our goal tomorrow is specifically, *specifically*, to make it clear to him that he needs to go there. Not soon, not later. Then."

"Why?"

They'd explained this, but I felt stubborn. Maybe I didn't get it. Maybe I didn't feel like getting it.

"Every addict is always saying 'Tomorrow,'" Joe said. "'Tomorrow I'll quit. Tomorrow everything will change.' And that tomorrow *stays* tomorrow. We're saying to your dad, '*Today*. Now. The hospital is waiting. Julie's ready to drive you there. Will you go?' That's what we'll ask."

"We've got everything set up," Julie said. "His boss is giving David time off."

"How long?"

"At least two weeks. Maybe a month."

"In the *hospital?*"

"Yes, Casey. We've talked about this."

"But what about me?"

"You'll stay with me," Julie said, patiently. "I've

got a pullout couch. There's space for you to do your homework and everything. I'll drive you to school every day, and pick you up at your house after I get off. It'll be all right."

"Your dad's health insurance will cover the hospitalization," Joe said. "We made sure."

"He may hit us with questions," Julie said, nodding earnestly at me. "We'll have answers."

I threw down my stick.

"So what if he tells everyone go to hell? Including me? This is *my dad* — the only parent I've got left around here. What's your answer for *that?*"

There was silence. No music in the bagel cafe.

"We realize you're the most at risk here," Julie said carefully.

"Hell, yes," Joe said as he sat up straight. "Casey, do you not want to do this?"

"No. I mean, yeah." I picked up the stick again. "I want to, but ... *I* don't know."

I looked at them. "I'm tired of doing so much stuff to take care of my dad. You know? It only makes things worse."

"But this isn't covering up or cleaning up," Julie said. "This is telling him the truth. This is offering him a way out."

"Yeah." I nodded. "Yeah. I know."

"Casey, listen to me," Joe said. "As families move

through the intervention process, I see them go through tremendous changes. It's like this energy gets built up from all the time people have held back against the truth. When they finally open up to what's really happening, it's like a dam breaks — and the energy pushes through. People start to change. I see it all the time."

Joe leaned over close, like it was just him and me.

"When you and I first met, you struck me as a boy trying his best to be good for his family," he said. "Now it's a few days later — just a few days, right? — and whoa, you're a teenager. Maybe a little confused, somewhat sarcastic, a little pissed off. Maybe more than a little. And I'm thinking, excellent! This is who you *are*. You've got a right to your life. Now let's help your dad take a big step in his life, too.

"Yes, there is risk here— and you don't have to do this, Casey," he said. "But you also need to know that addiction can be fatal. It's a path of dying inside — and it kills hundreds of thousands of people every year. We're trying to open a door to *life*. You both deserve to walk through it. Both of you."

I nodded. "I know. I want to do this. I do."

Joe sat back. "Okay," he said.

"We're going to do it in your house," Julie said. "Remember?"

"Yes."

"We need you to be there first, to let us in."

"Okay."

"Does your dad come home sober?" Joe asked. "Usually?"

"Unless it's Friday night, yeah. He doesn't start drinking till he gets home."

"All right, good. When he gets home, he parks his car where?"

"In the garage."

"Right," Joe said. "So we need you to go out there and bring him in. Our cars won't be anywhere in sight. He won't suspect, and we need you to make sure he comes through the door. Which door does he use?"

"From the garage. Into the hall by the kitchen."

"Okay. Now when you bring him into the kitchen, Julie will be waiting, and she'll take over. Your dad will be surprised, and he'll probably get defensive. Our goal is to keep him moving toward where we want him to go, which is the living room. Julie will introduce him to me, and I'll make sure he doesn't smell of alcohol. Or anything."

"I get it."

Joe said, "Is there anything else he might smell of?"

"Um ..." My face got warm. "He smokes weed sometimes."

Joe nodded. "Okay. Is he likely to do that in the car,

on the way home?"

"I don't think so. He does it in the garage."

"Right away?"

"No. Before ... before dinner."

"Okay. So I'll tell him some people are in the living room," Joe said. "We'll bring him in there. We'll show him where to sit."

"Where to *sit*?"

"Yeah. It's important that we manage this carefully," Joe said. "When the rest of us rehearse tonight, I'll tell everyone where to sit and in what order they'll speak. We're going to practice at your friend Oscar's house. We can't have you there, Casey. We need you to stick to your routine."

I shrugged. "I'm grounded anyway."

Julie's face crinkled. "Why?"

"Never mind."

But her forehead stayed wrinkled like that.

"Anyway," Joe said, "you'll be the last to speak. It's really critical that you be ready. Is your piece all set?"

"Uh, yeah. I wrote it."

"Good. Practice it tonight — and I want you to have the printout with you tomorrow. Be all set to read exactly what you wrote."

But I didn't think what I wrote said what there was to say any more. It seemed like I did it a long time ago. Before everything changed.

"You're the most important one, so you'll go last," Joe said. "We want you to add this to the end of your script: 'Dad, we've reserved a bed for you at Chestnut Ridge Hospital. Everything is taken care of. We'd like you to go there today. Will you go?'"

"*I* have to say that?"

Joe nodded. "It's best if it comes from you — if everything leads up to you saying that. Exactly that. Are you okay with it? Are you okay with all of this?"

I didn't know. I really didn't. Joe and Julie were looking at me now, waiting for me to say what *they* wanted me to say. But this was my life they were talking about. And if things didn't happen to go just right ... what would they say then? "Sorry. We really thought it might work." And they'd go off and leave me and my dad in the disaster. Or just me, if my dad told us all to shove it and took off.

Which he *could*.

They were waiting. I shrugged again.

"Okay," I said.

But I wasn't sure I meant it. I wasn't sure, right then, about anything.

18.

When I got home I didn't clean up. In the living room, last night's bottles were dark watchmen. Let them watch. My dad hadn't eaten breakfast in the morning, because I hadn't made any. I'd had cold cereal by the handful out of the box. I had no dishes to wash. I wouldn't have washed them if there were any.

I didn't know about food for tonight. I didn't know what would happen. I didn't really care.

I was in my room when I heard him come in from the garage. I heard the sound of grocery bags thumping onto the kitchen counter; then he went out again. Came back with more. I sagged, closed my eyes.

But the next sounds were not the clinking of six packs. They were more mixed, more unusual. And they went on for a while. Finally I eased open my door, stepped into the hall.

My dad was unloading groceries. A lot.

When I came into the kitchen, his eyes shied away as he kept on unloading. Milk, frozen french fries, lettuce, fudge pops. We used to like fudge pops.

"We needed a lot of stuff," he said. He was looking into the bags, then into the open fridge. "You know, I usually just get what we need for dinner. That's kind of dumb, I guess. I make so many trips."

He squinted at a bottle of shampoo, like he wasn't sure what to do with it. He set it aside, put his hands on his hips, and slowly looked up at me. It was like he was fighting against some invisible force.

"I'm gonna make a nice dinner," he said. "Gonna barbecue. Got spareribs, barbecue sauce, fries. We ... I haven't barbecued in a while, you know? We could eat outside."

He waited. I didn't say anything. He looked at me almost pleadingly, like he wanted me to say, "That's great, Dad. That's really great."

But I didn't. Because it wasn't. Everything started swirling up inside. I didn't know what to do; I got all twitchy.

"I'll get the barbecue ready," I said, starting for the garage door.

"Where is it?"

"In the garage. I'll bring it out back."

"I can help you."

"No! No, I'll do it."

In the garage, the barbecue was walled in by my dad's bicycle and a bunch of empty boxes left over from my mom and Shannon's move. The boxes just got piled up and left there. Clearing that stuff away kept me busy. I shifted boxes, moved the bike, and wheeled the barbecue, with its plastic wheels and propane tank, around to the back yard where it used to be. All summer it had never been outside.

When the food was ready, I brought out knives and forks, cleared some leaves off the picnic table, and set the utensils on it. I went back in and brought out the glasses and some lemonade Dad had bought. I rushed back and forth bringing plates, french fries, salad dressing. By then my dad was sitting down at the table. He was watching me. But I would do anything — anything — except sit down. With him. But I had to. I would have to.

Still standing, I looked at the table.

"Ketchup!"

"Huh?"

"We forgot ketchup," I said.

"Oh. Well ..."

"I'll go get it."

"Okay ..."

In the kitchen I leaned against the counter. I was breathing fast, and I felt so shaky inside. I had to settle down. But how could we sit together, sit and face each other? How could we talk, and ... not talk? My dad's face had almost looked desperate, like some stupid barbecue dinner had to make it all better. Or I had to make it all better.

But I couldn't. And I wasn't going to. So that, I realized, that was that.

I went outside and sat down. My dad's face lit up.

"Where's the *ketchup?*"

I looked at my empty hands. He started laughing. I looked up.

"You've got barbecue sauce on your chin," I said.

He swiped it off with his hand, then wiped his hand with his napkin.

"I'll get the ketchup," he said, grinning at me. "You eat."

I shrugged. As he walked away, I looked at his side of the table. He had a glass of lemonade.

I realized he was trying. Tonight, he was trying. But there was this intense, desperate energy he was putting out, like a force field: *Don't talk about it ... just make it okay. Pretend it's okay. Okay?*

Only it wasn't. I didn't believe in the lemonade. I knew the thing would pull him under; it would take him over again. It always did.

But then, when he came back and sat down with the ketchup, I looked at my dad and thought: *He's really not okay right now. He's stretched incredibly thin.*

Then I thought, *What'll happen tomorrow, when those people start to rip into him?*

Later, when dinner was finally over, when the dishes were brought in and our silence and desperate conversation-making and time-filling were finally done, my dad and I went in opposite directions. I think we were both relieved.

In my room I flipped open my laptop and printed out what I was supposed to say tomorrow, including the part they'd made me add today. I was looking at it, wondering how I could say any of this, when there was a tapping on the glass. I looked out, saw Oscar. And Tara.

I opened the window. "What are you guys *doing?*"

"These people are meeting at my house," Oscar said. "My dad went and got Tara so we could come harass you. We figured you might need a little harassment."

"Huh."

"You should see these people," he said. "It's like they're rehearsing a play, only without the main characters."

I looked at Tara.

"They told me about it," she said. "Oscar and his dad. I'm glad you're doing it."

"I don't know if I can," I said. "I don't know if I should."

"Whoa, man," Oscar said — "these people have

their *scripts*. They're practicing with that big guy — the horsey guy."

"Joe."

"Yeah. You see that guy's *hands?*"

"I know. Did you check out his car?"

Oscar's eyes bulged. "*Yeah.* He's got his stuff all piled on the back seat. Books, files, stacks of clothes. It's like a motel on wheels."

Tara was watching me.

"Can you do this?" she asked. "Really?"

"I thought I could, but ... I don't know if my dad can."

"But you've got to do something," she said. "You can't do nothing."

I nodded. "Definitely. Got to do something."

"Hey, it'll be a real-life experience," Oscar offered. "Possibly a new section for the Modern Library."

Tara's face brightened. "The what?"

"*Cap It Off*," Oscar said to me. "By U.R. Hammered."

I thought a second. "*Spark It Up*," I said. "By Willie B. High."

"Uh oh," he said.

"Wow," said Tara. "How long has this been going on?"

"Way too long," I said.

"Not long enough," said Oscar. He stuck his fist

through the window. I bumped it.

"Luck tomorrow," he said.

"Thanks. I'll need it."

"Just go for it," he said. "Whatever happens. Go for it."

They stepped backward, into the darkness. But Tara was still looking at me.

"I wish it was me," she said.

I nodded. "I know."

19.

Tuesday afternoon.

My hands were cold and shivery, like they couldn't grip. I sat on a kitchen counter, looking out the window at the empty driveway.

They were in the living room with Joe. I could hear them murmuring in there: Julie, Mr. Terry, Dr. Cavanaugh, Ms. Jacobs. They were sitting where Joe told them to sit, holding their sheets of paper with the words Joe had told them to write. They had saved two seats, one for my dad and one for me.

As soon as I saw the car pull in, I was supposed to call out, "He's here!" Then I was meant to go out to the garage and make sure he came inside, like he normally did, like everything was normal. From the kitchen Julie would steer him into the living room and introduce Joe, who'd sniff him like a police dog. If my dad passed the smell test, they would sit him on the couch next to Julie.

I was supposed to follow, take my seat, and wait my turn.

When my dad's Honda pulled in, the sounds of murmuring from the living room didn't stop or change. No one but me, so far, had noticed.

I slid off the counter and walked quickly down the hall. I opened the door to the garage, stepped through, and quietly pulled the door closed.

With a rumble the garage door started coming up. I rushed up and stuck out my foot, to break the electric-eye beam. The door stopped and I ducked under to the car, opened the passenger door and slid in.

My dad was looking at me.

"We have to go," I said.

"Huh?"

I glanced at the kitchen window, saw no faces. "Quick, okay? Just go."

"Where?"

"Just ... please! I'll explain."

He reached for the remote to send the garage door back down. I grabbed his arm. "Leave it," I said. "Please?"

He peered at me. "I assume there's a reason for this?"

"Uh huh."

"There better be." But he put the car in gear and

started backing out the driveway. I saw someone come to the living-room window.

My dad turned to face me. "Okay, where to?"

"That way." I pointed away from the house. "Quick!"

I had no idea where we were going.

On the back seat was a single paper bag. The bottom half looked full and square. So it had two six-packs.

This is it, I thought. *Whatever you do, go for it.* This is it.

The sign for the high school was coming up fast. "Here," I said. "Turn in here."

He swung the car quick and the car swerved; I bounced against the armrest. I remembered last Saturday, my head hitting that armrest behind me.

We came around back. Saw the stadium. His face got complicated.

"You want to be here," he said quietly.

"Yeah. This is good."

He stiffened, a little. Then he shrugged.

"Okay, no problem. Should I park? Or do you just want to take in the scenery?" He glanced at a teenage girl, jogging on the track.

"I think park," I said. "Maybe over there." I pointed over by the playground.

As he parked, his cell phone went off. He pulled it

out. Looked.

"It's your aunt," he said.

I sighed.

He said, "Hello? I'm ... fine. Huh? Actually, yeah. He's right here."

Looking puzzled again, he handed me the phone.

I said, "Hello?"

"Casey! What happened?"

"I'm not home, actually," I said in a calm voice. "I'm with my dad right now."

"I *know* you're not home. What are you *doing?*"

"We'll be home pretty soon, I think. I can call you when I get home, if that's okay."

"*Casey, what* are ..."

I pushed End. Handed him the phone.

He asked, "What's she want with you?"

I shrugged. The passenger door squeaked as I opened it.

"Come on," I said. "Leave the phone, okay?"

"What are you, the little dictator all of a sudden?"

"No," I said. "I just ... I just want us to hang out, okay? Walk the track or something."

He shrugged. Dropped the phone into the cupholder. "I hate that thing anyway," he said.

We walked past the playground. No way were we going there. I led us through the gate to the field.

The wooden ticket booth, the same one he'd dragged me past, was empty. It was a warm early evening; beyond the stadium, the trees were losing their leaves. Just a few people were on the track: that girl running alone, two high school kids walking along laughing, and a man and a woman jogging in track suits that looked identical, except his was red and hers was yellow.

I led us onto the track. The brown surface was a little spongy. I started walking. Basically, I had no plan.

He caught up with me. For a bit, we didn't say anything. As we came around the end zone, he looked across the field toward the other end, where the ambulance had been.

"I hope you don't think I enjoyed it," he said.

"What?"

"It's too bad that had to happen. But you deserved it."

I stopped dead. "What are you, kidding me?"

He stepped back. "No, I'm not kidding you. You broke the rules."

"What rules? You think we have *rules?*"

His face got squinty. "I'd watch my step right now, if I were you," he said.

That really annoyed me — but I could also see this wasn't going to work. If we got into an argument, we'd both have to win. It wouldn't work.

I started walking again. After a bit, he caught up, striding along.

"Casey, what are you trying to do here?"

"There's some stuff we need to talk about," I said.

He stopped dead. "Oh really," he said, behind me. "That's what you think."

"Yes," I said, stopping too. I turned to face him. "Honestly, I do."

"Well, maybe I don't," he said. "Maybe you had a lesson to learn and you learned it. End of discussion."

I just looked at him. He shrugged. Started walking back the other way.

"So you got in a little trouble," he said over his shoulder. "So face the consequences. It *might* be time you grew up a little."

I stood there staring. He was really starting to piss me off.

This time it was me catching up to him. We were both walking the wrong way on the track. I waited till the cute-suited couple had come up and passed us. My dad was ahead of me, walking fast. When I'd catch up, he'd walk faster.

"Look," I said to his back — "we have a problem, okay?"

"*You* have a problem."

"Yeah. You're right. I do," I said to his back. "Want

to know what it is?"

"Everything you say just digs that hole a little deeper."

"You don't realize it," I said, "because you don't *want* to realize it. Everyone's supposed to hide it. We're all supposed to pretend it's not happening. But it is ... Dad, will you stop? Dad. You're in a *bad situation*."

He stopped; I almost bumped into him. He turned and stepped backward. I couldn't read his face. I had no idea what would happen. But he folded his arms and gave me this tight little almost-mocking smile.

"All right," he said. "So. You needed to bring me out here. I get that. Maybe there's something you need to say. So, be my guest. Get it off your chest."

It was like he was daring me. *Go ahead, hit me. You can't hurt me. Try.*

So, it was weird, but ... I had this shot. One shot. I tried to remember what I'd written. What was on that paper?

"Remember what we used to do?" I blurted out.

"What we used to do?"

"Yeah." *Calm it down*, I thought. "You know, like ... when we'd go see the Red Sox."

"Fenway Park. Sure." He started walking again. Fast. I trotted alongside.

"Well, I loved that," I said. "And — that museum you took me to. When I was younger. Remember? A kids' museum. In Vermont."

"The Montshire. Sure. A science museum."

"Yeah, that's it. We went on a Saturday — it was raining," I said. "We had lunch together. In the back of an old general store."

"I remember that. They had a little room overlooking the river."

"Yeah! We ate our sandwiches. Then we stopped at a park. They had an old fire truck I could climb on. It was for kids, but it was a real old fire truck. Without wheels or equipment. Like sunk in the sand."

"Yep. You liked that."

"Yeah! And remember the souvenir shop across from Fenway Park?"

"Oh sure. The team shop." He laughed. "You thought you'd died and gone to heaven."

"Yeah. But ... see, in the last couple of years, it's like every time you say we're going to do something, something happens and we don't."

He looked at me squintily. "I don't know what you mean by *something happens*. I've got a lot to take care of right now. Sorry if I can't go sailing off to the *ball*park or the *kids'* museum every weekend."

"Yeah, but ... remember what happened two weekends ago? Saturday before last?"

He was walking and staring straight ahead. Inside I felt a mix of pissed-off and about to cry. In a low voice he said, "Are you suggesting I don't remember things?"

"No. I don't know. But that morning you said we could go see Dartmouth play football. I was so *psyched*. I thought, This is going to be great! But then ..."

He stopped dead. Hands on hips.

"Then, as I recall, we had plumbing trouble," he said. "Forgive me if I don't happen to be a pro*fess*ional plumber. Sorry if I'm not Superman in your eyes any more. It might be good if you *could* grow up a little."

That got the pissed-off part rising. I stopped. Took a deep breath.

"What *happened*," I said, "was that you tried to fix the faucet in the shower even though the lady in the store said you probably shouldn't. You didn't really listen to her. Then when the faucet didn't come loose right away you banged it with a hammer, and it broke into pieces. Then you got really mad, and you started drinking beer."

He stepped up close. "You better think about watching your mouth right now. All right?"

"You went into the living room and got drunk. That's what happened, Dad."

He stared at me wide-eyed, like he couldn't believe I was still talking. And I did not stop.

"I sat there for a long time in my room," I said. "I waited and waited, even though I knew we weren't going to any football game. I watched the clock go past kickoff time. I sat there and watched it, Dad."

He took a step back, looking stunned.

"That's what happens now, whenever you say we'll do something," I said. "You get mad about something, and then you get wasted. And we never get to go."

The about-to-cry part was rising up inside; I had to stop for a couple seconds while I pushed it back down. In those seconds, I think I missed my chance.

He turned and walked to the fence. The jogging girl dodged around him, then passed me with a nylony swish. My dad put his hands on the fence, looked up at the sky.

"Why don't you figure out how to get yourself home?" His voice was tight, like vibrating. "Because I'm not driving you, okay? So enjoy your last walk."

He was backing up. Starting to leave. "And when you do get home," he said, "just settle in and wait. Because when I get there ..."

"They're waiting for you, Dad.'"

He stopped. "What?"

"They're in the living room. They were waiting when you came home. If you go back now, they'll be there."

And I saw that I had wrecked it. The whole thing. I had wrecked it. He either wouldn't go home at all, now — he'd probably go to a bar — or he'd storm back there and throw them all out.

And then I *would* have to go home.

He gripped the fence rail. Stared out. "Casey, what in hell are you talking about?"

"They're there. Aunt Julie, Dr. Cavanaugh. Mr. Terry, and Ms. Jacobs."

"What?" He looked at me sharply. "Debbie *Jacobs*? Oliver Terry? Bill *Cavanaugh*?"

"Uh huh. And this guy named Joe. He's a professional."

"A professional what?"

"It doesn't matter. They're there to tell you that you've got to do something about how you're getting drunk and wasted all the time, or you might die."

I couldn't believe I'd said it. I knew it hadn't come out right. He stood there looking out at the empty field.

"I was supposed to be there too, Dad," I said. "But I just ... I felt like I wanted us to talk. Just us. You know?"

He pushed himself away from the fence, turned his back to me and started to walk. Stiff-legged as an angry marionette, the way he'd been that Saturday in the end zone, he stalked past the two teenagers. They stopped talking and turned to look at him.

He walked all the way around the end zone to the other side, where the bleachers are. He started climbing up those steps.

Most of the way up, he sat down. Right there in the empty grandstand. He just sat there, all by himself.

20.

It was the longest walk I ever took.

When I got to the bottom of the bleachers, my dad was sitting up there, staring straight ahead. He hadn't looked at me at all. I had no idea how he was.

The stairs led up between silvery rows of metal bleachers. I started up slowly; my feet felt so heavy. Every step made me tired.

When I was almost there, a couple rows down, he was staring out past me. He said, "So. You planned it all."

"What?"

"You and her. I should have known, the way she was taking you out. For 'ice cream,'" he said sneeringly. "The way she'd call and ask for you so *cool*. Like she was just being this good aunt."

I stood there.

"I should have known it about her," he said, biting

off the words. "But *you*."

He finally looked at me. His eyes were like nails.

"You're a selfish, disloyal little son of a bitch," he said. "You know that?"

My knees buckled. I held on, but stuff was coming up inside. Bad stuff, coming up fast. I held on hard.

"You go sneaking around behind *my* back," he spat out, "telling god knows *what* to these people. Here I am trying to hold what's left of my family together, and you two, who are supposed to be on *my side* — you go around turning people against me? Are you *kidding* me? Oh and by the way, you did an excellent job of picking just the people who can hurt me. Or get me fired. Nice *work*. I might not have a *job* tomorrow. Did that even occur to you?

"Or maybe ... maybe it *did* occur to you," he said. His eyes widened, like he was seeing the whole plot. "Maybe you two knew just what you were doing."

"Dad, come on. Why would I ..."

"Do not talk. You're done talking."

He took in a sharp breath, and looked away.

"I cannot believe you would do this. To *me*," he said. "With everything I do for you."

And that ... that was it.

"That is *bullshit!*" I shouted at him. "*This* is why Mom left, this is why you have no friends. You sit around and get pathetically wasted every single night —

and you think everyone *else* is the problem? It's not us, it's you — 'cause you're a freakin' *loser!*"

I had lost it completely. "You're not a dad, you're not *any*thing," I yelled at him. "You get disgustingly drunk and stoned and you act like *such* an asshole and *I'm* supposed to pick up for you? I'm supposed to clean everything up and wipe up your puke and cover up all this crap? Well you know what, I'm sick of it. I'm not *doing* it any more. Because you know what? *You make me sick!*"

He just looked at me; his mouth was hanging open. At that moment, I saw the horror in his eyes.

And then I could not believe what I had just said.

He stood up, and turned away. I wanted to say, *Dad ... Dad I just didn't want you to be hurt. I didn't want you to be humiliated. Can't you understand that?*

But I couldn't say that. I couldn't say anything. It wouldn't make sense now.

He took a step away. With his back to me, he said, "Tell those people to go home."

"I don't have a phone."

He shrugged. He walked across the row of bleachers, then down the aisle on the far side. At the bottom he turned the corner toward the main gate, without looking back — and now I couldn't see him any more.

I stood there sick to my stomach, just wishing I could take it back. Take it all back. Could I please have the last half hour of my life back? Please?

I didn't have any practice, I thought pleadingly, desperately. *I didn't know how to **do** it. It was too intense, it was too much, it was too ...*

I heard his car start. I heard him drive away.

21.

I sat down in the bleachers and stayed there. Didn't
know what to do. I couldn't move. It got darker and
darker, until it was night. Maybe I was hoping someone
would come for me. Maybe he would tell somebody I
was here, and they would come.

I didn't think that would happen, though. And it
didn't.

The people on the track all left. The stadium got
dark and empty. My butt hurt; this bleacher was hard.
I got up and walked slowly, stiffly, with nowhere to go,
down those steps. When I got to the bottom I walked
across the front of the grandstand and then past the
ticket booth. I thought, weirdly, *I could stay in there. It's
got a little roof.*

But I kept walking. And for a long time, that's all I
did. I walked, and walked ... and walked.

I couldn't go home, and it was dark and there was

nowhere else to go. After a while of walking I didn't know or care where I was; but it didn't matter, no one was looking for me and there was nowhere to go and maybe if I kept walking and walking I wouldn't have to feel so *bad*. Maybe I could walk faster or walk farther than all the bad feelings that had filled up inside, that were filling me completely, that wouldn't leave me alone.

I kept walking. It was dark and I was tired and there was nowhere to go. I don't know where I was, or where I went. I just kept walking because everything was hopeless and there was nowhere to go.

I was hopeless. If only I hadn't been stupid. If only I hadn't been a total idiot moron loser. If only I had done what I was supposed to do — or if I had thought of a *plan*, for god's sake.

If only I hadn't been me.

It was all my fault and my feet were really sore. My legs hurt bad. I walked and walked and walked but I couldn't leave it behind. None of it. I was walking with all of it and everything hurt, everything was sore and tired and hopeless and there was nowhere to go and it was all hopeless and everything hurt everywhere, and it was all my fault. *All* my fault.

I kept on walking and walking, on and on, just walking to nowhere in the dark.

I'm not sure how I got to the black path. I just noticed

I was on it. I looked around and felt a tiny relief to be someplace I knew, even though this was just an empty path through dark woods by a raised-up train track. I trudged along where Oscar and I had kicked fallen leaves the other day, when there was a world to live in, when there was a whole world I hadn't destroyed.

Then I was on the little bridge. Maybe my feet had brought me here. Maybe this was just the last place to go.

The last place.

I walked to the end of the bridge, and stepped over the rail.

In the dark it wasn't easy, finding my way down the sharp-edged shale on the bank. I could see the stream below. The water looked silvery as it slipped among the rocks.

Then I was down here. Under the bridge in the dark.

It was strange and different, it didn't feel like the safety spot at all. But I told myself there was nothing here. No bad noises, just the sounds of the water in the stream slipping by. I knew those sounds.

I lay back on my elbows and listened to the stream. It was dark under here, and the water lost its glimmery light coming through — but it was still the water.

The thoughts in my head settled down, a little. I guessed I could stay here. I couldn't walk any more. It wasn't very nice here, but at least no one would find me.

I turned on my side and shifted around, trying to find a comfortable place, but it was stony and hard. Every position was stony and hard, and hurt.

I'd been lying there for a while when from up on the path I heard voices.

My eyes popped open. I wasn't safe. If someone caught me under here, I'd really be caught. I thought about running but it made no sense. *Just let them go by.*

I stayed totally still. Didn't want to breathe.

The voices came closer. There was something about them. Then I heard:

"Here?"

"Yeah," said Oscar's voice. "Down there. Hey man, you down there?"

I didn't say anything. I couldn't say anything, I was way too ashamed. This was the only place I could be. The only place left.

A flashlight lit up the shale-glittery bank and the suddenly shining water. Now someone was coming down. As the person came down, silhouetted in the beam, its shape was thick. It had a hat.

Oscar crouched at the bottom, looked at me, and spread his hands like an apology. Then, still outlined in the beam, he looked up. He nodded.

The flashlight bobbed as the person holding it came down. When it got to the bottom, a much bigger shape looked in, and shined the light at me. I looked away.

"Tell you what," Joe said. "I am glad to see *you*."

Then he was shining the light back upward.

Someone else was coming down, this time slowly.

"Careful," Joe said, shining the light ... and now a form with longer hair was stooping alongside Joe and Oscar.

"Casey," Tara said. "Oh my god."

22.

Joe shone the beam around. It landed on the Bud Light box, above me on the bank, that we'd filled with the empty cans.

"Hey, still there!" Oscar said. "Really adds a nice touch."

Tara's head turned his way. "Is that *yours?*" she asked him.

"Don't be silly," Oscar said — "I have *taste*. Casey, on the other hand ... I mean, he'll pretty much drink anything."

They were looking at me, I could feel it. I didn't say anything. I was inside myself, in a deep dark hole.

Joe made a thing of settling himself. He was sitting now on the tilted bank, a big shape with knees bent and feet set down flat below him. He played the flashlight beam over the slip-slipping water. He offered me a drink of water, from a bottle he had. I shook my head.

"So," he said. "Long night."

I didn't say anything. Oscar and Tara went to sit down, too. Oscar said, "Oof."

"So. Casey," Joe said. "Any chance you could tell us what happened?"

I stared at the water. I couldn't say anything, I was down in the hole. They were waiting. But I was too far down.

After a while, Joe said, "I have to tell you, I wasn't totally surprised."

I looked at his shape looking at me. He shrugged.

"Something about it wasn't right for you, Casey — that got more and more clear," Joe said. "And hey, whatever happened, it's probably what needed to happen."

I shook my head hard. No. *No.* In the silence was the sound of the water slipping past.

Finally Joe said, "Well, okay. Here's what we know. You and your dad took off. When Julie reached you on your dad's phone, she said you sounded like you needed some space. Like you were trying to do something. And anyway, we had no choice — so we waited. We hoped for the best. After an hour or so, your dad called.

"It was a really short conversation," Joe said. "Actually not a conversation at all. He told her 'Thank you, go home, goodbye,' and he hung up. Julie could hear people talking in the background."

So he went to the bar, I thought as I slid deeper in the hole.

"We left your house," Joe said. "Your aunt, Oscar's dad, and me — we went over to the Terrys'. At this point we were pretty worried about you. When your dad called, to be honest, it sounded to Julie like he was in a bar."

I ... nodded.

"Right," Joe said. "And if that's where he was, we figured you were probably not with him. Since he was telling us to go home, we guessed that whatever had happened, whatever you'd tried to do, it had not gone ... well, it hadn't worked out perfectly. In that *moment.*"

All of a sudden my eyes were filling up, all wet. I hung my head, trying hard to stop that crap. I snuffled. Swiped at my eyes, my nose. It was gross.

"It's all right," Tara said. "We're just glad you're okay."

"*That's* for sure," said Joe. "Your aunt called your dad back a couple of times, but he wasn't answering. We had no other information. It got dark, and we were pretty stressed — you were out there somewhere. Your aunt was *very* concerned."

"I thought you'd come to my place," Oscar said. "You know you're welcome there, right?"

But I wasn't welcome anywhere. Only in my hole.

"When it got to be almost eleven o'clock," Joe said,

"your aunt said, 'That's it — I'm calling the police.' But we weren't sure what to *tell* the police. After all, you'd last been seen with the parent you live with. We had no real evidence that anything was wrong; but your aunt was frantic. She said, 'We have to do *some*thing.' She was ready to make the call."

Oscar cleared his throat. "So, um ... I told them there might be a place. One place we like to go to. I didn't want to give up the spot, man — but I was worried about you. Your aunt said we could come check. I was just hopin' you'd be here."

They all waited. I still didn't talk. I sort of wanted to, now. But I couldn't. I reached out for Joe's water bottle; he handed it to me. I took a drink.

Tara said, "I called Oscar's cell. I had to know what happened. He said they weren't sure, but they were going out looking for you. I asked them to pick me up first. I had to come, too."

"So here we are," Joe said. "And, Casey, if it's all right with you, I'm going to take a guess at what happened. I think you were worried about your dad being able to handle the intervention, so you diverted it. Maybe you figured just you could talk to him. Maybe you had a plan, maybe you acted on impulse. But the thing is, you *acted*.

"That's not such a terrible thing, Casey," Joe said carefully. "You love your dad, and I know you didn't want him hurt. So, okay. You took a chance."

The hole wasn't so deep now. I'd settled down a little inside it. My eyes were dry.

"Okay? So here's my next guess," Joe said. "I think you tried to talk to him, you really did try — but things got crazy. Maybe things kind of blew up."

My breath caught. Joe nodded.

"Right. So that happened. Then, I'm guessing your dad walked away. Maybe he told you to find your own way home, or something like that — but you felt bad, so you didn't go home. Who knows where you've been. Maybe you've been down here this whole time."

I shook my head.

"No?" he asked.

"Where'd you go, man?" asked Oscar.

"Casey. It's okay to talk," said Tara. In the dark, she covered my hand with hers. She asked, "Are you okay? Did he hit you, or hurt you or anything?"

I croaked out "No," shaking my head. They were waiting for more. Her hand was warm on mine. I wanted to speak ... but I couldn't.

Oscar asked, "Did he yell and stuff?"

I shook my head again.

"I ... got mad." My eyes filled up again; I swiped hard at them. *Don't.*

"Stuff came out, huh," Oscar said. "Like stuff he didn't want to hear."

"It's *not his fault*," I burst out. "He thought it was — like a plot. Like everyone was ganging up on him."

"Okay," Joe said. "He was defensive."

"He *hates* me now!" I was gasping. "It was horrible. It was *horrible!*"

Joe nodded. "I get that. What came up in you, came out strong. You feel bad. But that anger — I've been watching it build up in you, Casey. I think it's been building for a while. Are you sure it's so wrong that it came out?"

"Yes!"

"Why?"

"I don't ... I don't ... because I'm *stupid*," I said. "Because I wrecked everything and I'm *stupid*."

"No you're not," Tara said, her hand warm on mine. "You were mad because it wasn't fair. And it isn't fair. Parents should not act like kids. Parents should be *parents*."

"Hard to argue with that," Joe said. "So, Casey — I got one more guess. An educated guess. Okay if I take one last shot?"

He gave the flashlight to Oscar; then he raised his hands, poised for the free throw. I didn't smile. But I nodded.

"What I'm thinking is," he said, "that little speech I had you write — that was so careful, so *reasonable*. And that didn't cover it, did it? That speech did not let you have your anger. Our whole *plan* didn't let you have your anger — and you have a right to your anger. Why the hell shouldn't you? It's real, isn't it?

"I mean hey — I told you to be real, then I turned into Mister Control," Joe said. "I think that's when the thing started feeling not right to you. So you took action. *You* took a shot."

"And now he's gone," I said miserably. "Now it's all gone. I wrecked everything."

"No you didn't," Joe said. "Your dad's around, and you got some true stuff out. Maybe it came out a little hard and fast. Maybe it wasn't easy for your dad to hear. But that doesn't mean it was *wrong*."

Oscar played the flashlight beam over the water. Joe said, "Casey, I do these interventions all over New England — and each one plays out a little different. Sometimes the thing goes so smoothly, *so* much according to plan, that I start wondering if it's too smooth. And sometimes it is. Sometimes the addict or the alcoholic just goes inside, cooperates for now and waits it out. Maybe the treatment makes a difference — or maybe, soon as they can, they go right back to their stuff.

"Sometimes the addict tells us all to go to hell and walks away — but inside, they're shook up. They start thinking about what they heard," Joe said. "At the same time, the family has finally shared the truth with each other. They've broken through the silence, the denial, and the caretaking that, to be honest, only smooths the path for the alcoholic.

"When we describe the reality straight up, face to face, we're busting through walls that have been built up over years," Joe said. "That *changes* things. And it sounds to me like that's what you did. Any chance I could be right?"

"But it all went *wrong*."

"How do you know? It's up to your dad whether he faces it, maybe tonight, maybe down the road — but that's always how it is," Joe said. "It's always up to the addict whether to face this or not. But by bringing the truth to the surface, you have changed the situation. Can you see how much of what you did tonight was pretty damn brave?"

Tara squeezed my hand. The hole felt shallower, now. I could poke my head out, and start to look around.

Oscar said, "You guys have been playing Blind Man a long time. But you pulled the shades off. Man, you pulled 'em *off*."

He held his hat over his heart.

"I am totally proud of you," he said. "All my mentoring, my patient role-modeling, has finally paid off."

I whacked at him. "You are *so* weird."

"Hey — no hitting," he said. "No violence. Safety spot."

23.

It's been almost a month since that night. I've been staying with Oscar and his family, at least for now.

I don't know how things will work out, but my dad and I ... we're talking. Sort of. That night when we got back so late, Mr. Terry left a message on my dad's cell, telling him I was at their house and I was okay. My dad called back in the morning, after Oscar and I had gone to school. (Yeah, we went. I was a zombie, but Oscar ... was Oscar.)

At dinner that night, Mr. Terry said he and my dad had talked, for a minute on the phone.

"How was he?" I asked. "How is he?"

"I wish I could say I was able to tell," Oscar's dad said. "He was polite, but in a formal sort of way. He did want to make sure you are all right."

Mr. Terry is a nice man. "We are *soo* happy to have you here, Casey," he said to me in his musical accent.

Oscar's mom is American, and a lawyer; she's really busy with work and doesn't cook much. Oscar's dad works at home — he's some kind of software guy — and he cooks a lot. That first night we had shrimp and sausage with rice and it was good. I mean *really* good.

"I told him you are most welcome to stay with us," Oscar's dad said. "For as long as you like."

"Is he upset? Did he sound mad?"

"Well ... my guess is that his feelings and thoughts are all in a tangle right now. I think we're wise to give him a little space and time to sort them through. He knows we will take good care of you."

"Oh yeah — and speaking of that," Oscar said to his parents, "we also need to protect this guy from the women out there. He's got this stately mature girl *way* in love with him."

"Oh?" His mom's eyebrows went high. "Is she older?"

"You'd *think*."

Oscar chewed, and nodded. "You know what, she's okay," he said to me. "As your mentor I approve of the relationship."

"Imagine!" Mr. Terry threw back his head and laughed. "Such a relief!"

But I was worried. Oscar's mom saw it.

"It might be good if you wrote to him," she said. "An email. Just reach out. Let him know you want to be in touch."

"This is your attorney's advice — you must take it," Oscar's dad said with his big smile. "If you don't, she might double her fee!"

Oscar's mom shook her head. "You see what I live with?" she said to me.

"Oh, yes. Yes I do."

I sent him an email that night. I said I was okay at Oscar's, that I hoped he was okay. Then I wrote, "I'm sorry I got mad."

He wrote back even shorter.

"Glad you're all right," he wrote. "The back door is unlocked if you need anything. Make sure you tell your mom where you are."

I stared at that email for a long time. He didn't say he was sorry for anything. And when he said "Glad you're all right," was that sarcastic? Was he saying he wasn't all right? Part of me wanted to run back there and find out. Clean things up, take care of him.

But I didn't. I took a deep breath … and just didn't.

About a week later, my dad emailed and said, "I'm making burgers tomorrow night. If you feel like coming over." Again, I stared at his message, wondering: Is there an edge to "If you feel like coming over"? Should I go? Finally I decided to.

When I got there, feeling nervous about everything, the house was actually neat. I mean, fairly neat. No bottles, anyway. He was distant, but polite. We were both polite. He had a beer with dinner — he opened it in front of me, I'm pretty sure on purpose — but I only saw him drink the one.

We did talk, mostly about school and sports. He asked how things were going at the Terrys', and I said fine. I didn't want to say "Really great" and make him feel bad, but I also didn't want to pretend it wasn't nice over there. So I said fine. I wondered if he'd say, "Why don't you come back here?", but he didn't. He just said, "Huh."

That's as close as we came to talking about what happened. At all. Otherwise, it went okay.

Now, like I said, it's been almost a month. I go to the house for dinner about once a week, and we still talk politely about safe things. He asks about school and he does seem to want to know, which I think is good. After we eat, we clean up together, which is really nice. We're peaceful, basically, and we don't really talk. Some things he says, just little things, have that edge to them, like "If you feel like coming over." I think on some level he's staying mad at me, like holding on to that. Maybe that's how he's made sense of what happened — he's decided I was just mean and bad. Well, okay.

I do still feel bad about what I said, but not as bad

as I did. I apologized in my email for getting mad, but I'm not apologizing for telling the truth. Even if I said it badly, it's still the truth. And he's definitely not apologizing for anything.

So that's the way it is, at least for now.

He always drinks when I come over, and I always notice how many he has, which lately is two or three. I wonder how many more he has after I leave. But he does still seem to be cleaning up — I don't go over to so much of a mess. I hope that's a good sign. I hope he's thinking about things, like Joe said he might be. I don't know if he is. I wish we could talk about that stuff, but he seems determined not to.

I do feel like until we can talk about it, I'm not ready to go home. I'm not going back to pretending and covering up. Whatever happens. I'm just not.

I really like eating so well, at the Terrys'. And I like being in a house where ... I don't know ... where you can count on things, and where people sit back and laugh. It's not *tense* all the time. But it's also not my home. My dad and I ... whatever we've been, we are still family.

So that's how it is.

Joe and I email. We keep in touch. He's always off somewhere, working with someone new; Oscar and I call him the Lone Arranger. Joe says there are meetings, that almost any night my dad can walk into one. AA, you know? He says people can get clean and sober any time they're ready. It doesn't take a fancy intervention at all. But they have to be *ready*.

"I think he's getting there, working things through," Joe wrote me — "but it may take some time. The thing is, Casey, sometimes people have to fall a ways before they'll ask for help. We call it finding their bottom. Sometimes the best thing you can do, the only thing really, is take care of yourself, stop protecting them, and hope they'll come to that point of honesty soon. It's hard, but a lot of times it's what you have to do. It's good for you to stay connected, though. Let him know you're there."

I read that email over and over. I guessed he was right — this was what I had to do. He was also right that it wasn't easy. And I couldn't shake the feeling that I had let Joe down. I had failed him, not following the plan. But if I had, he dealt with failure better than anyone I'd ever known. That night I was in a deep, dark hole. He came and found a way, him and Oscar and Tara, for me to climb out.

And I was okay. I really was.

Tara and I did get our Revolution project done, back there. What we decided on was a skit in costume. She played Sam Adams — it was hilarious to see Tara pretend to be a guy — and I played a friend of his, drinking beer with his pal Sam the revolutionary in a pub. Yep, that's what we did. I had to do *some*thing edgy.

So we made tri-corner hats pretty badly out of construction paper, and we worked fairly hard to put together realistic manly outfits like colonial Boston patriots. We went to a thrift store, and we improvised. Tara turned out to be good at that. She found these old-style metal tankards — that's what you drank stuff in, back then — in her dad's party supplies at home. For our presentation in class, we filled the tankards with ginger ale and pretended to be sitting around in this vintage Boston tavern.

I asked old Sam, now that the Revolutionary War had started and he helped start it, how come he wasn't out there shooting a gun?

"I feel I can be more useful here," said Tara, and her fake-deep voice made some kids in the classroom chuckle. I'd had to really push her to pretend to drink beer in class — but after a while she realized it mattered to me, for some weird reason, so she just went for it. It was better than hatchets. And it was realistic, right? Old Sam was a beermaker, or something like that.

Anyway that's what she said. Then she added, "I am approximately 45 years old, also. Depending on what year this is." That got the class laughing.

"So," I said, "is this how it works? Old guys start the wars, then young people go out and get shot at?" At that point the class stopped laughing. We've got a couple of kids whose fathers or mothers are in Afghanistan. So this stopped everyone.

"Well," said Tara/Sam, "we all have our roles to play — but I am proud to have spoken up against King George and his henchmen." (She loved that word, "henchmen.") "And it *was* pretty dangerous. When you speak truth to power, you never know what may happen."

She tipped her tankard at me, when she said that. No one else knew why.

"To the rebellion," I said as we clinked tankards.

"Hear hear," said Tara/Sam. "To freedom."

We got A minuses. Tara said if we'd done the papier-maché map of Boston, we might have gotten As. But I didn't care — this was less work, and a whole lot more fun.

As for my mom, at first she was pretty worked up about what happened. I could hear her screeching on the phone with Mrs. Terry.

Oscar's dad winked at me. "Your attorney is smoothing the path," he said.

When I got on with her, my mom had settled down somewhat, but only somewhat. The first thing she said was, "How do you know he's all right? He's over there by himself. What if he's not all right?"

"Why did we pretend he was all right?" I asked. "All this time. How did that make things better?"

There was a long silence. I got worried she would freak out. But finally she said, "I ... guess I didn't know what else to do. I was trying so hard to keep everything together. Protect you kids. Protect him. Keep things ... I don't know. I didn't think you could understand."

"I do now," I said.

"I kept feeling like if I took care of everything, he'd get better," she said. "He'd pull himself together."

"Yeah!" I said. "And when he didn't, I felt like it was my fault."

"Yes," she said, "and I'd get so *mad* at him. I couldn't even talk with him after a while. He just drove me crazy."

There was another long silence.

"I guess ... I know it wasn't fair to put you in that situation, all by yourself," she finally said. "It wasn't fair to you."

"It's okay. I didn't mean to leave him alone," I said. "But that intervention thing was going to happen, and ... it got really complicated."

"I know," she said, "I've talked to your aunt. I know you tried. I do. Are you really all right?"

I liked how she asked that. Like she wanted to know.

"I am," I said. "Oscar's family is awesome."

"Oh, those men are characters! I told Nianna how

grateful I am. Do you have a room?"

"Yeah, the guest room. It's fine."

"Are you keeping it nice? Are you doing your laundry?"

"Yes, Mom. Thank you, Mom."

"Well, okay. I know you know how."

Another silence. Then she said, "I wish ... I guess ... I wish we could have been a little more honest. All along. But the situation, it ... kind of built up on us. You know?"

"Yeah. I know. I am going over there," I said. "I am checking up on him. I'm spending time."

"I wish it was different, Casey," she said, getting tearful now. "I wish this all had been so different."

"It's okay, Mom. It'll be okay."

"Well ... I hope so. I hope it will be." I could hear her sniffling. "Um ... talk to your sister, okay? She ... she wants to talk to you."

My sister? "Uh ... okay."

Shannon was all breathless. "Did you *do* that?" she said. "Did you *really?*"

"I don't know. I guess."

She wanted to know the whole story. So I told her, pretty much.

"Wow," she said finally. "You are *crazy!*"

"Oh, hey thanks."

"No, but listen — I talked to him," she said. "He

205

thinks you've got this *anger* problem. Like it's so strange, how you've suddenly out of nowhere got this problem. Like there's no reason for it except your weirdness."

"Right."

"I didn't argue about the weirdness, of course," she said. "But still."

I sighed. I didn't have an answer.

"Well," she said, "so? If he can't hear it yet, that's his problem. But you *told* him."

"Not well."

"But you *did*," she said. "Maybe one day he'll wake up and he'll get it. Maybe he already gets it, he just doesn't want to admit it. But if you didn't do this, I mean, who *knows* what would've happened? He was not going in a good direction."

You have no idea, I thought — but I'd never heard my sister talk like this. Everything had always been about her, like it always had to be. Maybe Joe was right. Maybe, in some way, things were changing.

"You know you can come live here," Shannon said. "You know that, right?"

"Yeah, I guess. But I've got school and stuff. And I don't want to leave him alone."

"Oh, I know," she said. "Mom would be *totally* lost if I wasn't here."

Well, that's my sister. And that's my family.

I wish I could say I completely know how the story ends. I wish I could say I didn't still feel slightly like an idiot. I wish I could have handled things perfectly and all.

But you know what, I did try.

One Saturday afternoon, I went back to the spot. I'd told the Terrys I was going to the library, and I was — the black path led that way. The library was just past the train station. I was reading a lot now, and needed more books. And I was going to meet Tara after.

But on the way, I stopped at the little bridge.

I stood there a while, looking around and thinking. I didn't climb down. The safety spot, down below ... it felt like that was part of my past, now. Or maybe it was part of me. Why it had ever been a special place in our childhoods, mine and Oscar's — this grubby little space under a bridge — I didn't know, really. But I think we felt like nobody would bother us down there — like we could play our games, turning over rocks for fluorescent newts and later making up Modern Library titles, and lying around talking and laughing as long as we wanted to. It was our spot.

Now things felt different. We were teenagers, and teenagers hang out under bridges for different reasons. Like with the Bud Light box. Maybe that's how people try to get that special feeling back, the feeling kids have

of being a little bit magic; I don't know. But no matter
how other people messed with it, whatever else happened
down there, for us our spot would always be innocent,
like this old safe place from when we were kids.

I leaned against the railing and looked down at the
water going by. I thought how that night, even when
nothing else was there with me, the water was. That had
been part of what we'd liked, being under the bridge
as kids: whatever we'd be doing, talking and laughing
or just hanging out, the water would be going by. In
the summer we'd stick our feet in it sometimes. It made
the place feel cool. Sometimes the water was high,
sometimes it was medium, sometimes it was low. But it
was always there.

I stood looking a while, then I understood it was
time to go. Sometimes you have to move on, you know?
It's a little sad, but it helps to know there are things
you'll always remember. As I stood on the bridge, I
knew that however this all worked out, with my family
and in my life, I would never forget how that night
down there I felt so all alone. I *was* all alone. And then,
all of a sudden, I wasn't.

It's not like I was moving away or anything ... but
things were different now. It was all right that they
were different. So in my mind, as I pushed off from the
railing, I sort of said goodbye. And thanks.

And then I walked on to the library.

Acknowledgments

The Prince of Denial is a newly reimagined version of a novel I first wrote some years ago, that was published in 2001 as *Raising the Shades*. For the vital help she gave me in developing this new project, I am grateful to Dory Rachel, my longtime good friend in New Jersey. Dory has given her life to the addiction recovery movement, and has helped a great number of suffering people find hope and turn their lives around. As we brainstormed Casey's story, she drew on and contributed her deep knowledge and experience — and whatever this book has become, it wouldn't have got there without her.

I'm also grateful to Patty Worsham, a master high-school English teacher in Virginia who read and critiqued the manuscript; to Lois Wood, a retired editor from Dartmouth College, in New Hampshire, who gave it an expert copyedit; to Debra Duffey and her eighth grade students in Michigan, for their excellent critiques; and to middle-school teachers Kat Kirst, in Texas, and Mark Domeier, in Minnesota, for their hawk-eyed proofreading. Thanks to Sarah-Lee Terrat of Yelodog Design in Waterbury Center, Vermont, for her powerful linoleum-cut artwork; and to Tim Newcomb, who did the fine book cover and page design at Newcomb

Studios in Montpelier.

Thanks especially to my wife Cary, who read the manuscript and offered several insightful ideas that did a lot to shape the final story — and for much more than that. It's in the home we have made together, with my stepson Nate and, when he can be with us, my grown son Brad, that I have been able to do this work more happily and wholeheartedly than ever before. My gratitude to my family is deeper than I can say.

Thank you, finally, to everyone who has encouraged me and responded to my books on my visits to middle schools, and through other communications these past several years. I'm a writer with rare good luck: I get to meet my readers, learn a bit about them when I can, and hear their thoughts, questions, and ideas many weeks of the year. When I'm asked by middle schoolers what inspires me, I say, "Well, you do!"

And it's true. So thanks to everyone I've met for the inspiration of their smiles and handshakes, their questions and messages, their enthusiasm and honesty. Thanks especially to all the young readers who have shared with me something of their struggles, their dreams, and their lives.

Doug Wilhelm
Weybridge, Vermont